All I Want For Christmas Is A Werewolf

LIANA BROOKS

OTHER WORKS

HEROES AND VILLAINS

Even Villains Fall In Love
Even Villains Go To The Movies
Even Villains Have Interns
Even Villains Play The Hero (books 1 – 3 omnibus)
The Polar Terror

FLEET OF MALIK

Bodies In Motion
Change of Momentum
For Every Action (forthcoming)

SHORTER WORKS

All I Want For Christmas Is A Werewolf
Fey Lights
Prime Sensations
Darkness and Good

Find other works by the author at
www.lianabrooks.com

All I Want For Christmas Is A

Werewolf

LIANA BROOKS

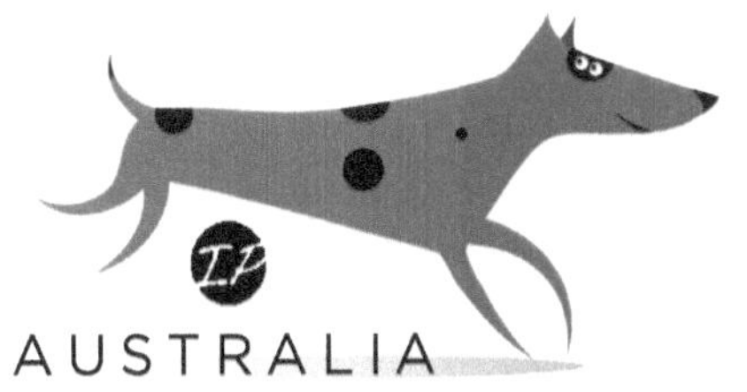

AUSTRALIA

Print ISBN: 978-1-925825-48-0
eBook ISBN: 9781393928959

www.inkprintpress.com

National Library of Australia Cataloguing-in-Publication Data
Brooks, Liana 1982—
All I Want For Christmas Is A Werewolf
180 p.   cm.
ISBN: 978-1-925825-48-0
Inkprint Press, Canberra, Australia
1. Fiction—Romance—Paranormal—Shifters 2. Fiction—Romance—Holiday 3. Fiction—Romance—Workplace 4. Fiction—Holidays

Summary: All Delinna Farmer wants is a family. But since Christmas miracles like that aren't real, she'll settle for a werewolf.

First Edition: December 2019

Cover design © Inkprint Press.

For all the people who don't want to go home for the holidays.

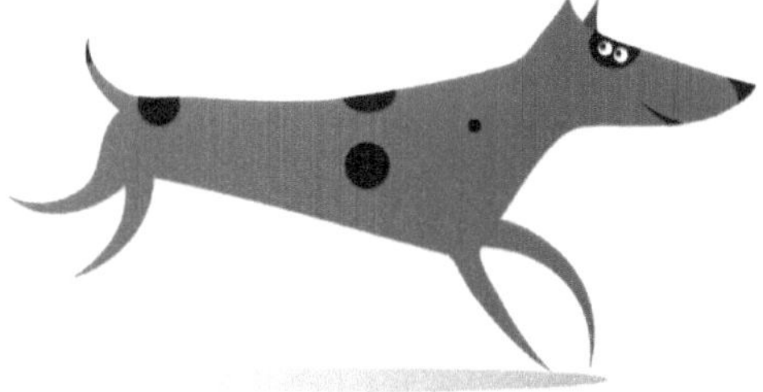

ALL I WANT FOR CHRISTMAS IS A WEREWOLF

THERE WAS MISTLETOE OVER MY DESK. HONEST TO goodness mistletoe hanging over the remains of my Halloween festivities. The Great Pumpkin was now overshadowed by a hemiparasitic shrub.

When I'd left for a conference two hours ago, my desk had been a bastion against the winter holidays. A snow-free island in an otherwise elegantly decorated office suite dedicated to art.

The gallery's front foyer with the dark wood paneling and over-stuffed pine-green tub chairs was now displaying glass and metal snowflakes in dazzling designs.

The main negotiating room, with the long table suitable for a fleet of lawyers, had a festive Seasons Greetings banner with pine trees and bright red birds signed by various Miami athletes.

The hall had garlands, multi-colored lights, and occasionally holiday music blaring out of incautiously opened offices.

But this?

This monstrous greenery was not supposed to touch my space.

Elegant Miami's main art gallery across the MacArthur Causeway was a glittering gem of holiday art. But over here, at the offices on Miami Beach that had been selected specifically to be near my boss's favorite house, things were toned down. This was where Elegant Miami hid the nitty gritty details of business. It was the safe space for the sales people that spent all day on the phone with overseas clients; it was the home base of the style teams who went and decorated Miami palaces with carefully curated art from around the world; it was a soulless sovereignty of the contracts office where Maureen and I made sure every jot and tittle were in place.

Tittle was one of my co-worker's favorite words. It means the dot over a lower case I or J, but it sounds funny. Stuck in an L-shaped, linoleum-floored concrete bunker with two high windows that looked at the neighboring building a foot away and that always smelled of nail polish and mildew, we took our fun where we could find it.

But I drew the line at plastic Naughty Santa window clings blocking the little sunlight available. Being held hostage by forced holiday cheer was not part of my paycheck.

"Happy holidays, Del!" Maureen jumped out from behind my desk wearing a bright blue sweater with silver bells, dancing elves, and snowflakes. The bell at the end of her bright pink Santa hat with pole dancing elves jingled as she stilled.

I stared, carefully counting to ten in every language I could remember, willing the other half the contracts team to vanish. It wasn't enough. Maureen and her seasonal cheer remained where they were.

"Don't you love it? I'm going to spray some fake snow too!" She pointed around at the sad, red tinsel garlands hanging off the black filing cabinets and the tiny palm tree that was sagging under a strand of rainbow lights.

"That's really not necessary," I said carefully circling around the hazardous airspace of the parasitic plant of unwanted kisses.

What was Maureen even thinking? Who on earth was I going to kiss here? It was against my personal policy to kiss clients or married people. That left Rafael Kane, office grinch, as the only possible target of unwanted contact.

Granted, he was a hot and sexy Office Grinch, but he was also the person voted most likely to ruin a party. He didn't chitchat. He didn't get distracted. He didn't waste time talking to coworkers, going to long Friday lunches, or building friendships.

Rafael Kane went to work, smiled for his clients only, and made Elegant Miami over fifteen percent of our yearly profit. We all loved him for his sales acumen, and stunning good looks, but no one around here considered him a friend.

Very early on, I'd tried. But Rafael Kane had taken one look at me, snarled like I'd stabbed his grandma, and avoided me ever since.

Which suited me just fine.

I frowned. If Maureen thought there was any chance of an office romance, my desk would look like an ad for the Great Bridal Expo. I needed tiny white seed pearls and chiffon as much as I needed mistletoe, which was about as much as a shark needed a tuba.

My idea of a good date was streaming a good murder mystery. I liked crime shows, creepy horror movies, and all things Halloween. People joked that I was a pagan, but that wasn't exactly true. I just loved the idea of magic. It made sense to me.

I should have loved the idea of Santa, except I can't remember a time I wasn't poor, and Santa doesn't visit poor kids.

December was my own personal hell. No winter solstice bonfire would ever be big enough to burn away all my anger at the forced cheer, demand for gifts, and unseasonable expectations.

I wasn't making New Year's Resolutions, I did that on my birthday in July.

I wasn't meeting anyone under the mistletoe, I wasn't that desperate.

I wasn't going to participate in the annual gift exchange, because somehow I always wound up with the bar of soap stolen from the pay-by-the-hour motel down the street.

I would be skipping the party, hitting the white sand beaches of Miami with a pink drink in hand, and spending my three days off catching up on N.W. Gehson's *Serial Killerz* series.

Maureen moved out from behind my desk and pouted. All of five-foot-nothing, she was a cute, apple-shaped woman with sunset pink hair and perpetually purple lips from a permanent makeup choice she made thirty years ago when she was twenty-one, drunk, and planning to be an exotic dancer all her life.[1]

In the bright blue sweater, she looked like the world's glummest Sugar Plum Fairy. She was holding a shiny blue paper with the words "All I Want For The Holidays" and a blank space for a holiday wish on it.

If I ignored the paper, I might escape further holiday interrogations.

"I... I was just trying to be nice!" A huge tear shimmered in her eye.

"I know." I patted her shoulder and tried very hard not to look at the tattoo peeking above her collar that HR insisted she keep covered during work hours. "But I don't like Christmas."

---

[1] She still dances under the name Cotton Candy every other Friday down at the Sugar Strip on 4th, if you're wondering.

"This year is going to be different!" Maureen assured, her smile turning on like a floodlight in turtle season. "I figured out why you don't like Christmas."

"Because it's a commercial farce to celebrate capitalism?"

"No, silly! Because you're single! No one's giving you the good gifts." She winked and tried to bump me with her hip, but since her head only comes up to my shoulder even in kitten heels, it didn't quite work.

I scooted around her and into my three-sided box of an office.

There were sparkly confetti snowflakes covering the nameplate that had been a gift from one of my favorite metal-work artists.

Delinna Farmer was not a name that deserved to have snow on it. Especially fake snow.

Shaking the snow off the metal cut-out of my name, I smiled up at Maureen. "Really, Maureen, I'm fine."

"You will be!" She pulled a scroll of candy pink paper out of her cleavage so it unrolled in a long, curling list. "This is Auntie Maureen's list of acceptable bachelors in the greater Miami area."

"Maureen," I said, sitting down and giving her my very best glare, "if Rafael Kane is mentioned even once on that list, I will murder you. Right here and now. There will be blood all over your dancing elf sweater. No jury will convict me."

She rolled her eyes. "Tried that. Obviously there's chemistry there, but Rafe could have chemistry with a doorknob, so it doesn't matter." She put the list of names—written in pink and purple ink—on my desk. "Names. Numbers. Histories. Sizes."

"Siz—Oh!" I covered my mouth. "Sweet mother of pearl! Maureen! This is so invasive!" I crumpled the list up and dropped it in the recycling bin.

"A girl's got to know..."

"I do not need to know anyone's sizes!" I shouted as the door to the contracts office opened and the devil himself walked in.

Rafael's brown eyes went wide, his tan face frozen in a rictus of horror.

"I'm not participating in the company Christmas party and I'm not ordering the shirts," I said loudly, willing Maureen to play along. Rafael might be the office grinch, but nobody gossiped as much as his people in the sales department. If he even guessed at the content of Maureen's list, I'd have every art gallery employee and intern in the greater Miami area sending me extra details.

Maureen, oblivious to the threat of Dick Pic Armageddon, crossed her arms over her ample chest. "Why not? What's wrong with the holiday party?"

"Because..." I scrambled for an excuse that wouldn't insult Maureen's party planning. "...I'm seeing someone."

Rafael snorted in amusement as he shook his head and walked to our copy machine by the door.

The sales department had a better one, one that could print posters and banners, but it was broken and the sales associates had been bouncing in and out of the contracts office all week. There was nothing like the holidays to convince the obscenely wealthy to drop hundreds of thousands of dollars on art.

"Oh, sweetie," Maureen said, grabbing my arm and leaning in for a sideways hug as she ignored Rafael. "You don't need to lie."

"I'm not," I lied. "I am in a relationship. And I think it's serious. We're talking about moving in together."

From the copier Rafael gave me a look of disbelief that said, *No one would ever live with you.*

Maureen patted my hand with a tiny sigh of pity. "Let me guess. His name is Nick 'The Closer' Claus and you ordered him from the toys department at Lady Things downtown? I've met him too." Her smile was wicked. "But he doesn't count as a dinner date."

Too. Much. Information.

Closing my eyes, I focused on the filing list I needed to finish today. Anything to get the image of my middle-aged co-worker gleefully bouncing through the adult toy store out of my head.

In my imagination, she wore a frilled pink skirt that barely covered her ample thighs. I shuddered.

My only option was to lie more, or to hope Rafael would step in to help me. "Maureen—"

"No!" Rafael shouted from across the room. "No more. Not until I leave. I do not need to hear this. Let me finish. Please. Five more pages!"

Just for that I wanted to play dirty, but encouraging Maureen would give me a heart attack. There was only one course of action left...

"I'm getting a dog," I said before the dick pics became porno subscriptions in my stocking. "I've been visiting the shelters and I'm planning to adopt one over the holidays."

Maureen's shoulders sagged. "Honey, that does not count."

"A dog will be more loyal than any man will!" I drew myself up, a furious dark queen with a mask of rage perfected after years of studying every campy Halloween vampire movie ever. Morticia Addams, eat your heart out. "Probably more loyal than a woman, too. It'll love me, wait for me, and cuddle with me while I watch horror movies in December. A dog won't make me watch cheesy Christmas specials. A dog will go for walks on the beach with me. A dog will be happy eating whatever I cook—"

"A dog should have a high-protein diet."

Maureen and I both turned to stare.

Had Rafael Kane actually joined a conversation that wasn't about sales? After all these years?

"Do you like dogs?" Maureen asked politely, reverting back to Sweet Office Eccentric like a chameleon. "You've never mentioned them."

Rafael stared at the wall behind the copier as he

realized his mistake. His body went rigid and I swear I saw a shiver of terror shimmy through him. He knew Maureen would never let him escape now.

"My mother raised dogs when I was growing up." He finished his copy work and turned to glare at me. "I've seen the stuff you eat for lunch, Del. Do the world a favor and stick to stuffed animals and battery-operated toys. A dog deserves better." He opened his mouth as if he were going to continue, then snapped it shut and marched out, back stiff.

Maureen hummed happily. "He has such a nice tush!"

"Maureen!" I smacked her arm.

"What? I'm married, not dead. I can look."

"We're at work."

"Quitting time was eight minutes ago. I can lust after people off the clock."

"You are a dirty old woman."

"Yes I am," she said proudly.

I rolled my eyes and remembered why I'd come back in. "I need to get my water bottles. I keep forgetting them." Nine of them sat in a row by my spare shoes.

"Oh, is that what happened?" Maureen asked. "I thought you'd decided to decorate with them. Maybe make a shrine to your beloved *agua*."

"Ha ha, funny." I grabbed a big bag with the name of a local farmer's stall on it and stuffed the water bottles inside. "The winter wonderland stuff... Can you keep it off my desk?"

Maureen pouted again.

"Please? I'll bring you some of those spiced pecans you like." If the bodega had a BOGO sale going on. If it wasn't buy-one-get-one, I wasn't sharing.

Her eyes went wide with delight. "Consider it gone. I will leave your corner a natural wasteland of bones, ghouls, and whatever that thing is," she said pointing to my Zany Zombie bobblehead.

"Thank you." I packed up and went home to research animal shelters. If I was going to be forced to participate in the holidays, I deserved to have someone who was happy to see me every day.

Surely I could get a dog for Christmas. It couldn't be that hard.

THE BEACH WAS NICE. TRITE, BUT TRUE. WHITE SAND sloped gently toward tropical, turquoise water and a fading blue sky. Pink and purple coquina clams dotted the tide line. Occasionally there was a shimmer of light under the waves as a slippery marine creature neared the surface and dove away again.

Here on the east coast the sun didn't sink over the waves, night rose. A stark, engulfing darkness surging up from the eastern horizon and gobbling the light. I breathed it in, the smell of briny ocean and tropical flowers with a hint of smoke and metal.

Exhaling, I let out the stress of the day.

It was quiet, because it was the last Tuesday before Christmas. The tourists hadn't arrived yet and all the locals were somewhere partying, or shopping, or whatever big groups of people did in the days leading up to family holidays.

My memories of holidays involved bonfires, tailgating, and screaming.

I'm not entirely sure when that happened, exactly. Most of my early life is a blur of disconnected images and emotions.

There was a car accident when I was seventeen, almost eighteen. I was in the hospital for my high school graduation, still having trouble forming sentences, and then I was eighteen and on my own.

My parents were dead… Possibly.

I'd been in the back seat of the car and we'd been hit from behind, that much I knew from the police report I'd memorized in the hospital.

The two adults spoke with the police briefly, gave their first names, and were supposed to follow the ambulance to the hospital.

Derry O. and Kitty Farmer had never shown up.

When the police had gone to the apartment listed on my driver's license, the place was empty and back rent was due. The landlord said she'd never met the family who lived there, but there were bills stacked up to several different names: Madra Hubbard, Jack and Jillian Hill, Missy Moffet, Jackson Sprat, Tommy Tucker, Lucy Locquett, Tom Piperson, Wynnie Nod.

My driver's license said Delinna Farmer. It kept with the nursery rhyme theme,[2] even if it didn't appear on any monitoring system outside the Florida DMV and the records of Cyprus Bay High School where I'd transferred in October of my senior year.

Even there, the office staff found a note with the words "Mom is bringing in the records next Tues" in the friendly, cursive writing of one of the elderly staff members who'd had an unfortunate stroke two weeks after I arrived.

I sat above the high tide line and stared out at the Atlantic Ocean as the sky changed from purple to black.

Early on, when I'd restarted life, I'd wanted my family to come find me. It would have been an appropriate holiday miracle. The kind you saw on TV.

But they'd never come.

Not to the hospital.

Not to find me at the homeless shelter, where I spent the summer after high school.

Not to my college graduation, when I finally finished it seven years later.

It was heartbreaking at first, to hope and dream, but I got over it.

No one was coming to rescue me. Whatever problems I had, they were mine alone.

I'd survived.

Alone.

---

[2] Delinna, as in dell, the farmer in a.

A seagull landed nearby and watched me hopefully with beady, yellow eyes.

"I've got nothing."

The bird squawked in disappointment and flew off to find someone willing to feed it.

I pulled my knees in tight and folded my arms as the lights turned on along the boardwalk. This was the secret reason I let Maureen and everyone else think I hated winter. Even if the weather wasn't that cold and most of our office were the amiable sort of atheist, I didn't want another reminder that seventeen years' worth of family time had been destroyed by a stupid drunk driver. Or that I was going to spend another miserable family holiday without family.

The little sniffle that followed I was going to pretend was the start of a seasonal cold.

I was not crying, darnit.

I was an adult. A big, tough adult who liked scary movies and soccer and monsters. I didn't cry because I was unwanted. A broken past didn't mean I couldn't have a better future.

As I was very definitely not crying, sitting on the cool sand while the ocean shushed away in front of me, something ran me over. Something that smelled like low tide and wet fur.

I tumbled to the ground, rolled to my side on the white sand, and looked up at the largest dog I'd ever seen on this side of town. It was a huge black brute with a silver belly, chocolate brown eyes, and gleaming white teeth.

Staying calm, I sat up and held out a fist for the dog to sniff.

The dog ignored it and instead pounced forward, managing to land with its legs over mine and its nose nuzzling my neck.

I fell back into the sand, fending off a friendly dog. "That tickles!" I giggled and pushed on its chest.

The dog grinned at me but didn't move.

"Can I pet you?"

It stuck its head under my hand and leaned in in a beautifully canine invitation to touch, its thick fur soft and warm.

"Who do you belong to?" I murmured.

The dog dropped to the sand and rolled to its—his—back, tongue lolling out.

"You're too well-groomed to be a stray." I looked around but didn't see anyone else on the abandoned beach. "Are you a tourist puppy?"

That would make sense. He'd probably come with his family and was staying at one of the beach rentals.

I rubbed his tummy for a few minutes and stood up. "Come on, let's find your people." My stomach growled. "And then I need dinner."

Rafael's horrified expression when I mentioned feeding a pet dog came back to haunt me.

I could cook. Really.

The basics at any rate.

It was just that I never found a *reason* to cook much of anything. Living alone meant eating alone, and eating alone was boring.

The dog rubbed against my leg.

Its head came up to my hip, and I patted it. "Come on. You need your people." We moved off down the beach, back toward the road—and people. "I don't even have kibble at my house."

Or bread.

Or ramen.

Or any of the basic essentials for life, unless water and kiwi fruit counted.

I wasn't even sure my fridge was plugged in, to be honest. I'd unplugged it for a little spring cleaning back in April and never really gotten around to plugging it back in.

That was going to have to change if I wanted a dog.

Did I, though? I hadn't even asked myself that when I'd run in fear from Maureen's list of well-sized men. It was an excuse.

But with the big, friendly black dog rubbing against my leg and trying to keep his ear under my hand, I could see the advantage. It would be nice to have someone happy to see me.

Maureen always looked at me with pity. The rest of the office acted like I was a free-range stack of paperwork come to haunt them. And the rest of the world didn't care if I were dead or alive.

Up off the sand and across the dune bridge, we turned the corner onto Ocean Drive. This time of year, half the condos were filled with Snow Birds, and the other half were available for rent. None of them looked like they had been vacated by a large dog though.

There were little giveaways in situations like this, like broken screen doors, open windows, or owners shouting for their lost pup.

Suddenly the dog, who'd been glued to my side, sprinted off along 5th, heading west to A1A.

"We're not running that far," I called after the dog with a sigh. Once I was home from work I didn't cross the bridge unless there was a hurricane coming, Cat 4 or higher.[3]

The dog lifted its ears, looked pointedly back at me, and continued its dash.

The enticing aroma of a truck promising Cuban food on the corner almost lured me away, but I chased after the dog. Food was important. Lives were more important. I could come back for dinner, but I couldn't save the dog if he got hit by a car.

He dodged down Meridian and then jumped over the low stone wall, dashing over the crabgrass lawn to barrel into the house.

326. The golden numbers on the gray stone gatepost burned into my brain as I ran past the open wrought-iron gate. Who knew. It might be important if I got shot for breaking and entering.

"Hello?" I skidded to a stop outside the open door to the house. "Hi. Hola? I'm... That's not my dog? Is

---

[3] As far as I knew, I'd lived in Miami my entire life, and I did not run from weak hurricanes.

it your dog? Is anyone there?" Pushing the door open, I looked into the shadows of the quiet house, waiting for someone to shout.

There was silence and then a dog barked. Something crashed in the house.

"Please don't shoot me! I'm trying to get the dog." I walked up to the open door, told myself that the best option was to close it and run for my life. But I couldn't leave the dog. Or the poor owners of the house who would come home to that black monster locked in there. I banged my fist on the door. "Hello! I'm walking in! Please don't shoot me."

This was going to be on the evening news. I just knew it.

The house was tastefully decorated, not ostentatious, but someone with an eye for art had created a serene oasis in the chaos south of 5th. Driftwood sculptures and paintings from local artists were staged around the main living room and down the long hall. There were the classic acrylics and watercolors you found hanging in the local cafes and in the boardwalk art shops. All of them leaned toward the stormy blue end of the color spectrum but with pops of yellow, orange, and bright green that perfectly captured the spirit of Miami.

I recognized several as being by artists our firm represented in the main living area. It was nice they'd found a good home.

By the front door, hung so it could be seen from the living room and the upstairs balcony, was my favorite painting of all: *The Storm In Her Eye*. On a canvas longer than I was tall, the artist had captured the front edge of a storm cutting across the bay. A stunning acrylic painting with bright sails and clouds so gray they looked like they would thunder right off the canvas.

I could *feel* the hurricane behind it.

And I was seriously tempted to just pick it up and walk out with it.

It was only a few blocks to my apartment. Not that I had a wall big enough for it, but I could give up my bed.

At least it was being appreciated here and wasn't stuffed in some collector's vault, forgotten and alone. This house felt lived in. It wasn't a rental and it wasn't like my studio a few blocks away, where I had a box-store bed, a couple of cheap prints, and some PVC tubing filling in for the missing closet.

The sound of bare feet hitting the tile floor behind me reminded me that I was breaking and entering.

I spun fast enough to make myself dizzy and found myself staring at a shirtless Rafael Kane.

Closing my eyes, I told my racing heart that I was hallucinating. Things like this did not happen to me. I was nice a girl who did not have to deal with the devil afterhours.

Opening my eyes, I looked down at the white tile of the floor. There were bare, brown feet. Check. muscular legs and white towel. Check. Abs... *Oh wow...* Very nice abs.

Broad shoulders, yum. Mouth, not bad. Eyes, chocolate brown. Hair, black.

…Rafael Kane. Check.

"Hi."

He lifted his eyebrows. "Hi."

"This is not what it looks like."

"What do you think it looks like?"

Bad. It looked very bad. "I was chasing a dog."

"Uh-huh." He didn't sound convinced.

"Big, black dog. He ran in here and I heard something crash."

Rafael leaned back to look around the corner.

I leaned too and saw the screen door of the kitchen hanging off the doorframe like a drunk at closing time. "Oh. I guess… I guess he kept going?"

"Was this the dog you were adopting?" Rafael sounded dubious.

"No. No." I shook my head. "Probably not. Unless he's a stray. But I don't think he is. I found him on the beach and he ran this way. I thought I should try to help him find his family." Way to sound pathetic. I looked away, stubbornly keeping my hands at my sides so I didn't cross my arms and reveal how pathetic I felt. If Rafael had even an inkling of respect for me, I'd just ground it into the mud.

He didn't say anything.

My teeth ground together. "Right. And with that I'll be leaving. I have… dinner to cook." That sounded plausible. My stomach growled again. Lunch had been six hours ago.

"Do you *know* how to cook?" Rafael's low tenor voice was filled with doubt.

"Yes." Technically true, if microwaving counted as cooking.

He narrowed his eyes in suspicion. "You always come to work with those box lunches from the bodega."

And he always came with a carefully portioned lunch filled with strange grains, lean proteins, and fresh fruit.

"I believe in shopping local."

Rafael stretched and sighed with a little frown that, at least at work, meant he was debating whether to argue with someone or not. More than one aspiring sales associate had seen that look just before they were told to pack their desk. Brown eyes looked me up and down. Rafe raised a questioning eyebrow. "Want to eat at El Mago De Las Fritas? They have their food truck parked up the street for another hour and I was going to go eat there tonight anyway."

I looked at his towel confusion. Had I chased a dog into an alternate reality? Was that even possible?

"Del?" Rafael snapped his fingers. "Delinna?"

I shook my head.

"No dinner?"

"Dinner yes, but you…" No. I was not going to point out he was undressed. "I'm confused." Being blunt has always been one of my hobbies. "Why are you being nice to me?"

Rafael shrugged a broad shoulder in a way that made the light play over his abs in a distracting fashion. *The Storm In Her Eye* wasn't the only piece of million-dollar art in the room. "Because I want to."

"You don't like me."

The look he gave me should have been framed for posterity with a title like *Hot Guy Meets Clueless Person*. I could feel my IQ dropping the longer he stared. As if I'd never measure up to his standard of perfection.

"This isn't about whether I like you or not. If I feed you, you'll go home instead of chasing some random dog into strangers' houses."

I put my hands on my hips. "That's not fair. He was a very sweet dog."

"Who is out playing in Miami traffic."

"And you're not exactly a stranger."

He stilled, watching me intently. "Did you know this was my house when you ran in?"

I stifled a nervous laugh. "Um… no. But it worked out, right?"

Rafael ran a hand through his black hair and turned away. "I'm going to put on clothes. If you leave, close the door." He walked off as if he didn't care what I did.

Typical. I sniffed.

The bayside painting tempted me again.

"Hands off the painting, Del," Rafael called from upstairs, as if he could read my mind.

Unfair.

I glared after him. "Why do you have it?"

"Because I bought it." He walked back down wearing ripped jeans and pulling a white t-shirt on that did nothing to downplay his good looks. There were sandals waiting by the door. "I like it."

"So do I! I saw the sketches but it didn't even go on the market!" I'd been waiting for it, saving for it, hoping to hang it in my eventual, maybe, one-day living room. Working in contracts didn't earn me a commission like the people in sales got, but I staged a few homes and received bonuses for referrals. My savings account was the only healthy thing in my life.

Rafael shrugged, looking like the arrogant SOB he was. "Should have moved faster."

"I hate you," I grumbled, crossing my arms. My heart was pounding in my chest. I wanted to go home, to curl up safe under my blankets and escape all the conflicting emotions.

Rafael Kane was safe because he was distant. But this? This was not distant.

"Do you hate me too much for me to pay for dinner?" he asked, a teasing smile playing at the corners of his mouth.

Well... There were principles, and then there was free food. "Not that much," I allowed—very, very grudgingly.

Food was a requirement, right? That made it safe. The food truck was neutral territory, not his, not mine, just a place two co-workers might wind up. We could eat near each other, chat a little to be polite, and it wouldn't mean anything.

Rafael snorted in amusement and nodded toward the door. "Next time you come in, shoes off outside."

"There won't be a next time," I promised as I stepped outside, suddenly hyper aware of my sandy white flipflops.

Rafael stepped right behind me, chest pressing against my back as he locked the door. "Yeah. Right. No next time." He winked as he brushed past me.

Holy mother of pearl! The devil was buying me dinner and unless I was totally mishearing things, it sounded like he wanted me to come back home with him afterward.

I put the back of my hand to my forehead. Maybe I was coming down with a cold after all. Or maybe it was a brain tumor.

Or maybe I was desperate for sex and he had a really nice body.

I watched Rafe walk down the sidewalk, remembering the rumor that he'd paid his way through college by modeling.

"Get a grip, Del," I muttered to myself.

He waited under a palm tree and I hurried to catch up, flipflops flapping on the sidewalk.

It was quiet for Miami. There was a steady hum of traffic in the distance, the low sound of voices and music, the smell of barbecue and cars, the distant sound of the ocean. The sun was setting on paradise, and for the first time in years I was walking to dinner with someone.

What a weird afternoon.

I should have stayed home and watched *Train To Busan* again. Weird days were made for classic zombie movies.

My phone rang, the opening strings of Mendelssohn's Violin Concerto E Minor Opus 64, which meant work. "Elegant Miami, this is Delinna in the contracts department, how may I help you?"

Rafe wrinkled his nose in disgust. "We're off work."

Taking a half second to hold my phone away I whispered, "I have overseas clients." And the boss was at dinner with a big spender, which meant I was on call.

"Delinna, darling!" The voice on the other end had the over-enthused tones of someone on their third martini. "This is Carson Vietti! How are you?"

A shiver ran down my spine. Vietti was my fourth least favorite client, a big spender who thought everything he saw was for sale. Last year he'd been relentless in his wooing, sending me flowers and offering to buy me a house in Coral Gables. Trouble with an ex-wife had taken him away overseas suddenly and I'd wished them a happy reconciliation.

If he was back in Miami, it meant Round Two hadn't worked out and Vietti was back on the prowl.

"I'm doing well, Mister Vietti," I said with a tight smile. "Is there something I can help you with tonight?"

I stopped at the corner of the street under a palm tree wrapped in white lights and motioned for Rafe to go on without me. If this went like I thought it would, I'd be calling a ride back to the office instead of eating a free dinner.

Rafe stayed beside me, hands in his pockets, expression unreadable.

Vietti continued. "You know that divine Suzanna piece? The blue one?"

"*Visions In Blue*?" Everyone knew the piece, we'd been getting calls and bids on it for weeks. "It's exquisite."

"I'm buying it!" Vietti said triumphantly. "Spoke to Suzanna just now and made her an offer she couldn't refuse."

Ugh. That meant paperwork. "When would you like the contract by?" I asked, fully expecting him to say within the hour.

"Tomorrow is good enough."

I sighed in relief. "Wonderful."

"But you need to come here!"

"Excuse me?" My angered shock wasn't enough to pierce the happy bubble of alcohol sheltering Vietti from the rest of the world, but it drew the attention of everyone on the street.

Several people frowned at Rafe and I grimaced in apology.

"Come here and celebrate!" Vietti was saying on the phone. "I'm buying dinner for everyone at the office!"

Putting on my smiliest voice, I wished I had the power to strangle people through the phone. Why wasn't there an app for that yet? "Mister Vietti, that sounds lovely, but I'm afraid I'll have to decline. I'm already committed for the evening."

Vietti muttered something incomprehensible.

There was a pause and then "Del?" in my boss's voice.

"Sir?"

Barros? Rafe mouthed.

I nodded. "What was that, sir?"

"I asked if you were with a client, Del," my boss said. "Vietti is a very important client, and unless you have an excellent reason to be away tonight, you are going to be at the Rockwell on Washington Avenue by the time they open."

In my head, I was saying prayers to whatever forgiving deity wanted to rescue me from a night of boozy, middle-aged men who wanted to tell me the same six stories all night in an attempt to flirt.

If I told Barros about Vietti, I could get out of it—probably—but Vietti would walk away from the sale and Suzanna would be in tears. It was unfair to punish a wonderful artist just because I didn't like the idea of Vietti possibly chasing me again.

He hadn't done anything wrong. Yet.

"Tell him you're with a potential client," Rafe said.

That was a good idea. With one minor flaw. I held the phone by my hip. "He'll ask what I'm selling."

"The driftwood table Martin is making."

Of course! The beautiful driftwood and sea glass

piece that I'd been coveting for months. Even the making-of photos were exquisite. Rafael had good taste—and so did several potential buyers who had emailed me when the article about the table had come out this week.

I was going to lose that table. I just knew it.

With a bitter smile, I lifted the phone. "Sir, I have someone interested in some of Martin's sea glass work."

"The table?" he guessed, the promise of millions giving him focus.

"Yes, sir."

"Wine them, dine them, and put it on the company card," Barros ordered. "Try to get their bid over two million."

Ha, not likely. Martin wasn't well known enough. "What's my commission?"

"Twelve percent," Barros said.

I laughed. Knowing what you're worth is always good business, and since I handled the contracts, I knew exactly what everyone in sales earned. I wasn't settling for half of what a junior sales associate made.

"Twenty-five," Barros countered.

"Sir, I'm working after hours for this deal." And that table was going to be hard to move. People were interested, but no one was offering because they weren't sure what they thought of practical, usable art.

"Thirty percent commission but only if you close the deal this week."

"Thank you, sir. Enjoy your evening with Mister Vietti." I ended the call and looked at the food truck in misery. Goodbye, delicious Cuban food. Goodbye, quiet evening. "Barros told me to put dinner on the company card. Where do you want to eat?"

Rafe looked up and down the street, then shrugged. "The food truck is good."

It smelled delicious, but it hardly counted as wining and dining. "If I get in trouble for this…"

"You won't. How much does Barros want you to sell the table for?"

"Two million."

"It's worth at least three."

"It's *avant garde* and unique," I said as we crossed the street. "None of our usual buyers are interested in it and the people calling in have only made tentative offers in the low thousands."

Rafe slowed by a temporary wooden table to look at the menu. "What do you—"

"Number four," I said without looking. I knew every food truck, bodega, and restaurant between South Pointe Pier and Dade Boulevard like I knew the complete works of Laelanie Larach.

He nodded and left me at the table while he ordered, coming back with an orange Fanta for me and grape one for himself.

"Three point five."

I took a sip of my drink and stared at him. "Three point five?"

"For Martin's table."

"Sure," I said. We could pretend like we were negotiating. "Three point five." What a nice daydream. I could picture that table in my house, with *The Storm In Her Eye* hanging in the living room.

If I closed my eyes, it looked an awful lot like Rafe's living room.

I sighed, and took another swig of Fanta. Well, it was a pretty dream. And like everything during the winter holiday season, it would never be anything more than a dream.

"So, do you have big plans for the holidays?" Rafe asked when it was obvious I wasn't in the mood to indulge his hypothetical sales scenario.

"Does rewatching four seasons of *Kingdom* and reading crossover fanfic that links *Train To Busan* with *Kingdom* count?"

Rafe narrowed his eyes as if he we were trying to interpret a foreign language and shook his head. "No."

"Do you even know what any of that is?" I asked as a runner dropped two recycled paper plates piled with food in front of us and zipped away.

"Twenty-seven hours of watching zombies in Korea and maybe a hundred pages of a good crossover fic. Maybe. I doubt it's more than a drabble."

I laughed, Fanta almost going up my nose. "You do not look like the kind of person who knows anything about fandoms."

"Really? In high school I was a big fan of *Teen Wolf*." He grinned; it only made him more handsome.

"Not. Possible." It would be easier to believe he'd acted in the *Teen Wolf* reboot.

He shrugged with a teasing smile tugging at his lips. "I was a scrawny, sarcastic kid who didn't fit in. It was perfect for me."

My eyes widened in delight. "Oh. My. Word. Rafael Kane, are you a closet geek?"

"Werewolves aren't geeky! And I'm not closeted." He tilted the neck of his bottle of soda at me. "I'm very bi and very comfortable with my sexuality, thank you." He lifted the bottle in a mock cheers.

I focused on my dinner while a million thoughts skipped through my brain. Rafael Kane liked werewolves? He liked horror? We had something in common? I stopped and pinched my leg.

Rafe raised his eyebrows in question.

"It's been a weird day. I thought I'd make sure I wasn't dreaming."

"Would dinner with me qualify as a good dream or a bad dream?"

"Weird," I said definitively. "You're not... dying or anything, are you?"

He stared at me for a long, uncomfortable minute. "Dying?"

"It's just, you're acting very strange. Out of character. You never talk to me at work. We're not friends. And, it's just..."

Rafael Kane was nothing more than a co-worker, but I couldn't handle a holiday tragedy. I cried over roadkill and dead fish on the beach; finding out a co-worker was dying made my chest feel tight with panic.

"I don't avoid *you*," Rafe said quietly. "I avoid Maureen. She's always eyeing me and I feel uncomfortable being ogled by someone older than my mother. And you're so tight-laced and all-business at work that I've never really had the chance to talk to you."

"Oh. So..."

"So I'm not dying."

"I have Zany Zombie on my desk. I'm not that straight-laced," I argued, tilting my bottle back at him. "You could have talked to me before."

He lifted his shoulder in a shrug. "You could have talked to me too."

Not possible. Rafe was the kind of person that made rooms light up. Everyone loved him, instantly. He was rude and stand-offish as a form of self-defense. If he smiled at a gallery opening, he wound up with more groupies than the artists.

A darker thought whispered doubts in my mind. "Is that why you invited me to dinner? To tell me I wasn't giving you enough attention?" I frowned.

"No, but when a beautiful woman walks into my house, I'm going to take the opportunity I'm given." Rafe rested his elbows on the table, breaching the no-fly zone between us. "It's not like I could talk to you at the company party on Friday."

"True." I nibbled on my pickled carrots in silence as I tried to think of anything else. December holidays were worse than cheap pickled jalapenos, bitter and bland.

Rafe pushed a side of fried plantains across the recyclable paper plate. "Are you okay?"

I nodded quickly.

"It's just, you seemed upset at work today. Chris The Secretary said you took your name out of the holiday gift exchange. He's heartbroken because he thinks you're going to quit." There was a hook in his statement, fishing for information.

"Quit?" I laughed. "Why would I? The job is good. I like it here. It's one bus away from my apartment."

"It's just that I keep trying to start a conversation and you keep killing every topic. So..." Rafe wrinkled his nose. "I know it's been a minute since I dated anyone, but usually I don't have this much trouble keeping a dialog going."

Considering I'd seen him charm the grumpiest of Miami elite into buying a teddy bear painting for three times the market value, I believed him. I nudged my empty Fanta bottle, staring at the damp ring it left behind on the table. "It's really not you. I'm a buzzkill this time of year. I just don't like winter holidays."

"Why not?" He sounded genuinely curious.

"Because they're for families and couples and groups. I don't have a group."

He nodded.

"You have a family, right?" I was sure he'd mentioned them before.

"Yeah, I'm the third of six kids. My parents and grandparents all live in Orlando. The furthest away anyone lives is my older sister in Tallahassee."

"I bet they love and adore you and welcome you with open arms."

Another nod.

I met his eyes. "Do you like it?" I wanted him to say he hated it. It was an ugly thing to think, but jealousy is an ugly emotion.

"They love me unconditionally," Rafe said.

"Must be nice." Dinner had lost its flavor. I pushed it away.

Rafe shook his head. "What about your friends? I'm sure you have some."

"Military assignment to Guam, tracking rare insects in Madagascar, undercover FBI, one who says she's a civil rights lawyer in Africa but might be CIA, and then Sherri died last year. Breast cancer. We're close but, um, they're not the kind of people you can call any time of day. I get emails every other month or so." I shrugged. "It's cool. People grow up. They have lives. They have kids. Life is busy."

The dark, desperate thoughts that had haunted me just after the car accident tip-toed through the shadows in my mind, whispering that I should walk away. If I left now, I couldn't be abandoned again. I wouldn't be forgotten because of life, or kids, or chemo.

"That's why I'm getting a dog," I said to silence the whispers.

"To make you feel loved?"

"Dogs are amazing animals." I stabbed at my remaining bite of meat. "They love you unconditionally. They don't care what you watch or which holidays you like. They don't pressure you to do anything but go for walks and maybe a run on the beach, which I already like doing. A dog would be perfect for me..." I nodded. "Besides, you can't adopt a werewolf."

Rafe laughed as he took my empty plate and bottle. "You want a werewolf?"

"Who wouldn't?" I followed him as he dropped the trash in the recycling bin.

"Somehow I pictured you for the vampire type. Smooth. Cold to the touch. Rich." He managed to put a spin on his words so they were sexy and threatening all at once.

"Ewww! No." I shook my head. "Vampires make the worst boyfriends. Have you ever read the books? They're always going on about what their mortal lover can do for them. *I need you to be human. You make me better. Your blood is my favorite drug.* All the emotional labor is on the non-vampire. Skip!"

Rafe crossed his arms and shook his head. "You thought about this?"

I shot him a brief grin. "Of course I did. In college my friends and I came up with a supernatural ranking of everyone on campus. Vampires are the ones who need you to do all the work. Zombies are the ones who say they want you for your brain, or your style, or your sense of humor, but they really want is this idea of you they made up in their head. They don't really want you.

"Ghosts are, you know, the ones who vanish with no warning." I waved vaguely at the distance. "Demons are the ones who seem great and then get steadily worse and worse. Angels are the ones who are amazing but just don't love you back. Fun to be with, but they always break your heart." I nodded decisively. "Werewolves are the best."

"Really?" He sounded more amused than skeptical.

The hot meal and happy memories of a time when my friends actually talked to me regularly made me smile. "Of course werewolves are the best! They're completely loyal, wonderfully protective, they want you to be happy, they are always hot as Miami in August, and they can turn into a dog that loves you no matter what. There's no downside."

"Expect for the possibility they might try to eat you."

"Well, there's eating someone and then there's *eating* someone." I bit my lip to hide my grin.

Rafe's dark cheeks turned a reddish-copper as he blushed. "Oh, gah—" He pursed his lips together and then started laughing. "You've been around Maureen too much."

"No, I'm a healthy adult who likes sex. Is that wrong?"

He shook his head. "No, of course not. It's just…"

"TMI?" Latent embarrassment reared its head. "Sorry. I have no filters after work. There should probably be a warning in the employee handbook."

"There is one, actually. The sales training manual has a sticky note on the page about contracts that warns everyone to not mention sex, strippers, or dating anywhere near the contracts office. Maureen has a sixth sense. You mention one of those and she appears like an evil genie with bad life advice."

I nodded. "Yeah. I know. Trust me: *I know*. Life with Maureen is—" I sighed. "She's not all bad."

"No, no. She's just... Maureen."

"Very Maureen," I agreed. I ran my hands along my jeans and looked up at the dark sky. "So, um, thank you for dinner. It was nice to talk to you outside the office. And, uh, I guess I'll see you at work tomorrow."

Rafe nodded. "Want me to walk you home?"

I shook my head. "I'm good. It's just down the block and this neighborhood is safe." Safer than where I'd been living a few years ago, anyway. But a life of Miami living had probably warped my views of what was safe.

"Okay then. Goodnight, Del."

"Goodnight, Rafe." I stepped away with a little wave and only looked back once. Maureen was right when she said he had a nice tush, but that wasn't the only part worth looking at.

"Do you know what mistletoe is?" I asked Maureen casually as I glared at the fake plant still hanging over my desk. "It's an obligate hemiparasite. It leeches nutrients from its host, slowly killing them over many long, presumably painful years. It's toxic."

Maureen looked up at the decoration mournfully. "It's Christmas-y."

"It's pagan-y," I corrected with a stubborn glare. "The Celts believed the white berries represented male fertility and semen. The Romans hung it over the door at Saturnalia as a symbol of peace and love. Which, when you consider the Romans conquered and enslaved the better parts of three continents, makes a lot of sense that their pick for a peaceful plant is a poisonous parasite."

My co-worker's jingle bell earrings tinkled as she tipped her head to the side.

I raised my eyebrows. "Translation: Why is it still over my desk?"

"I couldn't find the step ladder!" Maureen's bottom lip wobbled as her eyes filled with alligator tears.

I put my hands on my hips. "Maureen. If you don't find a way to take this down, the last thing people are ever going to hear about you is the headline, 'Local Woman Drowns In Riptide.'"

"Ah…" Rafael stood in the doorway to our office, hand poised to knock. "Is this a bad time?"

"No. Not at all." I dropped my bag by my desk and gathered a stack of papers so I could run like a terrified gazelle if anyone approached my desk and the dread plant hanging over it.

Maureen's eyes went wide as she sat down and suddenly became very busy with the contract pile she was reading through. Coward.

"I really don't want to be a party to murder," Rafe said.

"Do you know where the footstool is?"

He looked up at the mistletoe and over at Maureen with a scowl that she pretended to ignore.

"I want it gone before some idiot takes it for an invitation and I have to defend myself with my stapler," I explained, as calmly as I could considering the circumstances.

Running out of the office screaming because you're consumed by rage and regret isn't the way to secure a holiday bonus.

Rafe surveyed my desk, showing no reaction to my horror collectibles until his eye caught something out of my line of sight and his mouth twitched up into a smirk. "One dinner and you're already wedding planning?" he teased, voice pitched soft and low so Maureen couldn't hear him.

I glanced behind me and saw the bridal magazine with a two-page spread of an up-and-coming actress from Nowheresville, Alabama, wearing a sparkling-white mermaid wedding gown. Of course he'd noticed the full-figured woman falling out of her dress. "Remember the client whose piece went missing after the show in Amsterdam?"

"Is that her?" Rafe frowned, but switched topics with admirable speed.

"No, but that might be her piece." I picked up the magazine and pointed to a golden statue in the background. There was a green striation barely visible that had caught the eye of our client. "It's hard to tell at this angle, but it's about the right size, and it's the right shade of green for a statue made of jasper, tiger's eye, and gold."

Rafe's eyebrows went up in appreciation. "Good catch."

"Not mine. A friend of the client noticed it, and the client called us. I'm trying to track down everyone involved in the photoshoot to see who staged it and if we can get a look at their inventory." I closed the magazine and tucked it out of sight under a folder. "Feel safe now?"

"No." Rafe's eyes caught mine as he grinned. "I'm a little disappointed."

"You think one dinner was going to sweep me off my feet?"

"Maybe..." He drew the word out as his grin widened.

I shook my head. "Maybe? Did you think I was desperate?"

"Maybe I just like women who like werewolves." Normally when people said that they were being sarcastic, or hoping I'd admit to a furry kink. Rafe made it sound like my love for horror movies was as sexy as the tiny pink bikini I wore in the summer.

My cheeks burned as I tried to hold back a smile. Using werewolves against me was definitely cheating. "Shouldn't you be at work, Kane?"

"I am at work." He stepped forward, moving perilously close to the no-fly zone under the mistletoe.

"Shouldn't you be doing something?" I asked as I edged away.

Maureen's office phone rang. "Maureen, Elegant Miami. Hello Mister Vietti. Of course your contract is ready. If you'll swing by my office on your way in—"

My gaze flew upward, glued to the hemiparasitic ball of unwanted kisses hanging overhead. If Vietti saw it, he'd take it as an invitation, and I couldn't assault a client without losing my job.

Rafe was watching me.

I made eye contact.

He reached up, snapped the wire holding the mistletoe like the sword of Damocles over my head, and hid it in his large fist.

"Del?" Maureen said.

I jumped with a little start and looked at her. "Hmmm? Did you need something?"

"I said Mister Vietti is here to talk about his contract."

"Good. Good! Of course. Thank you. Have Chris The Secretary show him on in." I risked a glance at Rafe's balled fist and mouthed, "Thank you."

"Just being a good co-worker," he murmured too low for anyone else to hear. "Vietti can get handsy."

Didn't I know it. Him and every other aging millionaire who came in here thinking that their wealth made them attractive no matter what age. Somehow, they'd never realized that this was Miami, and I worked with wealthy people all day long.

If I really wanted a sugar daddy, all it would take was rolling up my blue pencil skirt an inch or two and popping the top button off my silk blouse.

Rafe was watching my hands.

"What?"

"You're still holding the scissors and you look like you're going to stab someone," he whispered conspiratorially.

"Oh!" I dropped the scissors on my desk and put on my professional face. "Better?"

Rafe nodded.

Vietti walked in. He wasn't liver-spots-and-full-time-nurse old, but he was over retirement age and fooling no one with the black dye in his wispy hair.

"Delinna!" He held out his arms for a hug and kissed the air by my cheeks as his eyes focused on my chest.

Men like him were the reason I kept my shirts buttoned to the collar bone.

"Mister Vietti, how are you today?"

"All the better for seeing you, my dear. You're so pretty. Did you get your hair done?"

"Mmmm...." *Nope.* "New shampoo," I lied. "My stylist thought it would bring out the red highlights."

He had said no such thing, because I hadn't gone to a stylist since I was job searching. Most the time I went to the local cut-n-dry place for a ten-dollar trim and all the gossip I could stand.

Vietti preened at the idea of having flattered me.

I grabbed his contract off the printing tray and motioned for the door. "If you'll come this way, Mister Vietti, I'll show you to Mister Barros's office so we can sign."

"Perfect, perfect. I can't wait to get my hand on this painting. It's so..." his hands traced a figure eight in the air "...voluptuous."

"Mmmhmmm," I agreed politely, because it was my job.

We walked down the hall together, past rows of holiday wishes, and one caught my eye: 'All I want for Christmas is a kiss...' It was a fair approximation of my handwriting, with my name in Maureen's familiar, flowery handwriting at the top.

I was going to kill her.

Vietti grabbed my wrist.

My eyes went wide as I gently shook off the octogenarian.

"As soon as I've signed the contract, we're going out for drinks," Vietti said, ignoring my body language.

And the wish behind him, where I'd apparently written I wanted a kiss for Christmas.

In Maureen's handwriting.

Why? Why? *Why* had she done that?

"My treat. I had a very good year and I want to share." He winked at me.

"Ah—" Come on brain. Find an excuse. *Find an excuse!*

"Del!" Rafe's shout made me freeze and pivot.

"What?!?"

Rafe stood in the doorway to my office looking disinterested and slightly annoyed. "Where's the contract for the table?"

"The table? Martin's table?"

Rafe nodded as I heard the door to Barros's office open. Was Rafe serious?

Then again, did it matter if Rafe was serious if I got away from Vietti?

"Del, go get the contract sorted for Kane," Barros said. "I can help Mister Vietti from here. Carson, come in! How are you today?"

The contract for the painting was whisked from my hands and I was left alone in the hall, staring at Rafael Kane in bewilderment.

"You want a contract drawn up for Martin's table?" I walked briskly down the hall, my heels clicking on the cold, marble floor.

Rafe didn't move from the doorway as I stepped in, so I had to turn sideways and slide past him.

"Really?" I asked since Maureen had her headphones on and we were as close to alone as work allowed. "Or was this a distraction? I appreciate either but—"

"I offered you three point five for it."

I stared, aghast. "I thought you were joking! I mean, it's worth that much at least, and it'll be worth ten times that if he ever gets the attention he deserves, but you know he'd take a lower bid."

Rafe looked nonplussed. "It's worth three point five now. Martin undervalues his work. That doesn't mean I should. Besides, I earned a hefty percentage off the sale of the Levine estate. Why not reinvest in an art piece I love?"

Because I loved it too. I could feel myself pouting, just a little, as I sat down at my desk.

The shadow of Rafael Kane loomed over me. "Besides, I think I need some art that you can't carry out my front door."

"I wasn't going to steal *The Storm In Her Eye*!" I said primly. "I just thought it is all."

Rafe smiled. "Three point five for the table, Del. It'll look good by *The Storm*. If you want to visit, you know right where they are."

Yeah, behind his front door, guarded by a man who I couldn't figure out.

I licked my dry lips as he walked away. There was something more than generalized holiday stress short-circuiting my brain. It felt like Rafe was offering more than just a meal or a chance to see my favorite pieces of art.

More wasn't something I knew what to do with.

More meant losing touch. Missed phone calls. Canceled plans. Sitting alone because everyone else had a family emergency.

More meant goodbyes, and silences, and funerals.

More meant risking myself for someone's approval again and the chance of being rejected—again. Of being broken. Again.

Turning back to my desk, I viciously snipped all thoughts of *more* at the root.

I needed zombie movies and werewolves, not another heartbreak.

ONE OF THE BEST PARTS ABOUT HALLOWEEN IS THAT you never have old, white men telling you that *Die Hard* is a Halloween movie. Come Christmas time, every guy who thought Bruce Willis was the epitome of lit (cool? groovy? toasty? what slang did they even use back then?) tries to corner you by asking if you think *Die Hard* is a Christmas movie.

If I say I don't believe in Christmas, do I go to hell?

Or was I already there? It certainly felt like eternal torture after five hours on the phone with a client in Lisbon who was fussing over what to buy her wife for her birthday. Five hours and she finally told me the birthday was in May and she'd call back in April.

I wanted to set my phone on fire.

Then Barros stopped me in the hall to ask about *Die Hard*. Two junior associates joined in on the fun, insisting on reciting lines.

By the time five o'clock rolled around, I was ready to cut the next person who talked to me, and I still had a bus ride to survive.

Slamming my water bottles into my backpack with extra vigor, I gave Maureen the death glare of No Talking so she'd know to leave me alone or else.

She got the hint and hid behind her desk, industriously starting emails for the next day.

I scanned my work space, dusted off one last foil snowflake, and marched out to catch the bus.

Vietti was waiting for me, cherry-red convertible idling in the parking lot like the ozone layer wasn't in danger and the sea levels weren't threatening to turn my beachside apartment into an artificial reef. "Del!" He held up a hand. "Want a ride?"

"Oh, Mister Vietti..." How did you say *'Hell No'* to a customer who was bringing in regular sales? "You didn't need to wait for me. I can take the bus."

"No need. I'll drive you home. We could stop for a little dinner first, if you wanted. Or vino at my place." The hard look in his eyes turned the suggestive smile into a cruel leer.

"I really couldn't. I—" I grabbed my phone from my bag like I'd heard it vibrate. "Excuse me, Mister Vietti." I put the phone to my ear. "Hello?"

The silence was a welcome reprieve.

"Right. Got it," I said to the imaginary person on the other end of the line. Flicking the phone off, I gave Vietti an apologetic smile. "Sorry. I need to go back in and handle something."

"I can wait."

"It could be all night. Why don't you head downtown? I'm sure there's someone who would love to party with you."

Vietti shook his head. "Del, why do you do this? We could have so much fun together."

"Oh, you could do so much better than me," I said with a self-depreciating smile. "I'm such a workaholic. And boring. Ask anyone."

He ran a smug, lecherous gaze over me. "I could make you fun."

"I don't like fun."

Did those words really leave my mouth?

Yes, they did.

And as long as the fun was with Vietti, I stood by that statement.

Giving him an apologetic wave, I slipped back into the office, mentally listing all the people I wanted to have fun with. No one came to mind. After a day like today, I wanted space. Lots of space.

Lots of quiet.

It would kill me after I'd unwound. In a few hours I'd be desperately lonely and wondering if I was destined to die alone, forever unloved.

But right now I needed to get away from every single living human before I punched someone in the throat.

"Del!" Maureen's screech caught me as I headed to the back door.

I pivoted slowly, imagining a rising minor chord and rushing wind behind me like I was in a movie. "What?"

"Martin is having a gallery showing."

"*What?!?!*"

Several glass vases in the foyer trembled in terror.

Three people ran from the sales office to the hall to see what the problem was.

Rafe was one of them. He looked between me and Maureen. "What happened?"

"Martin is hosting a gallery showing," I said, grinding my teeth hard enough that sparks should have been flying.

Rafe swore quietly in Spanish. "When?"

"Friday," Maureen said. "During the big company Christmas party. Remember last time he was left unattended?"

I shook my head in disgust. "He sold a piece for twenty bucks to some English tourist." Martin had no respect for his work. He just liked to have fun. If he was hungry, well, it was Miami, he could dumpster dive.

As one of those kids who'd lived off dumpster diving, I understood. You could live in Miami like that. But Martin deserved better.

Maureen widened her eyes and batted her three-hundred dollar false eyelashes at me. "Since you weren't planning on going to the company party..."

A little groan of despair whistled through my lips. "I hate showings. That's sales' problem. I just write up the contracts." If I did my job right, the only person I interacted with was the banker, and then only by email.

"Rafael…" Maureen switched to full Hot Mama mode, flashing him a flirty grin and winking.

Rafe seemed unmoved by the attempt at seduction.

"Please?" Maureen said just bit too breathlessly to be real.

"No." Rafe cut a look at me. "I have plans."

Probably a date with someone who didn't babble about werewolves and vampires. There was a little worm of jealousy twisting in my gut, but I was too tired to care.

"Send me the time and location," I said, capitulating. "I'll look at the details in the morning." I waved a tired goodbye to my co-workers and slogged off to the back door.

"The bus stop is the other way," Rafe said as the others vanished back to their desks to pack up.

I looked longingly at the front door. "Vietti is there too. And I don't want a ride home."

Rafe nodded. "Want company?"

I shook my head. "I need a good four hours of not dealing with people before I can be trusted not to stab someone. Thanks for the offer though." It was the best I could do.

"What would you do with a dog?" Rafe asked as he smiled. Maybe he understood how I felt.

"I would love it, and hug it, and pet it." I waited long enough for him to smirk and look away, but there was no witty quip to follow up. "No jokes about how you like to get petted too?"

Stunning brown eyes caught mine. "Not at work."

Right. Not at work. Our Rafe was a serious sales associate. "Night, Rafe."

"Goodnight, Del."

I took the back roads and alleys on the two mile trek to my house. And I wasn't entirely surprised—or upset—when the big black dog from the day before ran up to me a few blocks from where I'd last seen him the day before.

"Hey, puppy." I patted my thigh to invite him over.

He ran toward me and slid under my hand, stretching himself out so he got a whole-body pet.

"Were you being good today?" I scratched him under his chin. "Did you stay home like a good boy?"

The big black dog snuggled closer, almost pushing me off balance.

As I bent over, trying to keep myself from falling, the dog reached up and licked my face.

"Really now? I don't know where that tongue has been." But I didn't mind. I kept petting the dog as we walked the last little stretch to the main road. East and I headed home. West and I headed to Rafe's, which was near where the dog lived.

The dog turned west.

I almost followed.

Almost.

But Rafe deserved better company than me tonight, and I knew I didn't need anyone. I needed space. Maybe a good cry.

I needed to complete my holiday ritual of drinking hot cocoa and staring out at the street waiting for my family to appear until midnight.

Every year since I'd turned eighteen, I'd waited one night a year, the cocoa in my cup growing cold, watching the lights turn off and on in the morning light.

Waiting for someone to appear.

Some kids had empty stockings waiting to be filled. I had an empty heart.

The words to a Christmas song drifted through the open courtyard of the apartments. "He sees you if you're sleeping. He sees you when you're not."

Fear crawled up my spine like a heavy palmetto bug and all my muscles tensed. I hated that song the most. Every single time I heard it I went spiraling into anxiety attacks.

My feet moved automatically, sprinting up the three flights of cement steps until I was safe in my house behind a triple-locked door.

It was getting worse. Every holiday season I was getting worse.

Shedding bags and clothes, I discarded the smell of the office and stepped into the shower, scrubbing away the memory of carols and snowflakes and mistletoe with plumeria and plum shower gel.

Even in the hot steam of the shower I shivered.

I wanted to curl up in the corner and sob. It felt unfair, but under the unfairness were scabbed-over memories of pain, neglect, horror.

Real horror, not the manufactured stuff with zombies. Vampires and werewolves were a funny kind of horror. Zombies were hilarious and safe. You were allowed to fight back with zombies, kill them if you had to.

But somewhere at the back of the darkness in my brain, I knew there was a memory of a monster I couldn't kill. The accident had taken my memories, but not my instinctive reactions. The truth about my past was gone—maybe for the better—but the pain lurked, watching like creepy ol' Santa Claus, ready to beat me anytime an unknown trigger appeared.

Every holiday season made it worse.

Every attempt to create new, happy memories sent me spinning off into a set of reflective, self-destructive behaviors.

As I towel-dried my hair, I reviewed my work day.

I'd threatened Maureen over a decoration, almost insulted a very lucrative client, and practically bitten Rafe for offering to walk in the same direction with me.

He'd probably had to wait at the office to avoid running into me.

"Son of a biscuit, Delinna." I glared at my reflection in the apartment's single tiny round mirror hanging over the narrow bathroom sink. "Everyone is going to think you're crazy. This is why no one from college talks to you."

The girl staring back at me looked ready to cry, dark eyes rimmed with red.

"You keep scuttling your own happiness for people who you don't remember. Why? Does it really matter what happened?" I asked her. "Do you really want to find your family?"

I looked away, unable to even meet my reflection's eyes.

We both knew the truth. The holiday specials said you would find your family and your happily ever after. That was the narrative arc for any story that started with a beautiful but troubled girl who lost her memories on Christmas Eve.

But I didn't want to read that script.

I hadn't wanted my family back since—I had to pause and think—it had been years. The first year, yes, I'd expected them to come back. The second one I'd been on the street because I was too old for the foster system. I'd gotten into a shelter for Christmas and all they played were cheesy winter holiday movies while I drank watery hot chocolate next to a woman who was sixty and on the street because she couldn't afford to pay for her medicine and a house.

Her name was Stacy and she'd died before Valentine's Day. I'd only found out because there was a memorial reminder hung up at the soup kitchen.

But, for the day, Stacy said she'd adopt me, weird name and all. Her two boys didn't care what she did and never called. My parents didn't care what I did. We were the perfect match. And maybe that was my perfect holiday ending.

By the third year I was angry. Angry that Stacy had

died. Angry that I was spending another holiday break on the street because my scholarship didn't cover the cost of the dorm over any holidays. Angry that no one cared enough to look for me. Angry that my boss couldn't find room on the schedule for me during a lucrative waitressing season.

I'd been angry ever since.

Angry and scared.

I tossed my towel over the shower door to dry and pulled on a comfy pair of oversized pajama pants and my favorite zombie run t-shirt that was so threadbare it looked lacier than anything sold at the lingerie store. More comfortable too.

Grabbing the ever-present notebook from my nightstand (this one was shiny black with a stick figure vampire and the words *Fangs For The Memories*), I tucked myself into bed and started making a Pros and Cons list of finding my family.

Medical history was a pro. Finding out the truth about the long list of nursery rhyme names was a pro.

Everything else was a con.

Including the legal trouble people who had used nursery rhyme names were likely to cause. There was just no way they'd been on the up-and-up. From the way I swore—all sugar and biscuits—they were probably running some sort of church scam. Fake preachers maybe? Or joining congregations to get cash? Fake medical scams?

Who knew?

Not me!

Nor did I want to know, I realized as I looked at the very long Con list.

It had been nearly a decade since I'd been left alone in a hospital room with no memory of my name or family. I didn't need it now.

Which meant I wasn't in a holiday movie.

Or else that Christmas with Stacy had been the end-credits and I was drifting in the merry land of Happily Never After. An alarming thought.

I turned the page on my journal and started thinking of other movies where the character wakes up with amnesia. *Bourne Identity,* that was a good one. *Maze Runner* could be ruled out—Miami was sketchy at times but not exactly *Lord Of The Flies* meets *Murderbot Diaries. Wolverine...* I stretched my fingers to see if adamantium claws would pop out.

No such luck.

Open Grave, of course, but I doubted I was a serial killer. ...All right. I mostly doubted I was a serial killer. I thought about killing people, but that was a normal Miami reaction to things. I didn't *actually* ever hurt anyone.

Not a lot of good zombie movies with amnesia though.

Didn't mean there couldn't be a good dram-com about zombies and amnesia victims. *Oh! Warm Bodies*! The zombie had amnesia!

But I wasn't a zombie, and I really didn't want to be one. Eating brains to regain someone else's memories was eww.

Maybe a werewolf movie with amnesia? I couldn't think of one off the top of my head.[4] But that didn't mean I couldn't have a werewolf story.

It fit my current life script, right? Lonely girl with no memory. Soul-sucking job possibly working for vampires, or whatever people wanted to call Vietti and his ilk. Holiday loneliness creeping in. Big, black dog who wasn't exactly a wolf but wasn't exactly *not* a wolf either.

And where did Rafael Kane fit into it?

I tapped my ichor-green, sparkly gel pen on the journal as I thought.

Did Rafael Kane need to fit into this script?

The mental image I had of him—brown hair and eyes, soft lips, easy smile—made my libido chime in. I was a grown adult and, yes, dangit, Rafael Kane could fit in. Puppies were cute, but Rafe was sexy.

Sexy and he'd watched *Teen Wolf*. He'd hinted at being willing to watch zombie movies with me.

Plus, he had excellent taste in art.

I couldn't get a werewolf, but I could get a dog and a man, which was pretty darn close to werewolf.

No. Scratch COULD.

I could *maybe* get a dog and a man. Neither of those were done deals yet. I needed to find the big black dog or go find another wolfy-looking pup at the shelter. Then I needed to figure out how to get Rafe's

---

[4] Ha ha—zombie pun... I hope no one ever reads my journal...

attention in a positive way without tipping off Maureen that I was up to anything remotely sexy or salacious.

That sounded fairly impossible, actually.

Maybe I needed to revisit the whole brain-eating idea.

I rolled over in my bed and stared up at the mosquito netting and fairy lights.

I had a mostly-broken gray couch, a mattress piled onto cinder blocks and wooden pallets, posters and medals from zombie runs thumbtacked to my wall, and a fridge I hadn't plugged in since April. The bookcase was from a rummage sale after a hurricane, most of my art was posters or preliminary sketches from some of my local favorites. The only color came from the school of glass fish swimming across my window. How in the name of the Great Pumpkin was I going to convince someone as suave and sophisticated as Rafe to give me the time of day?

Step One: Never let him see my apartment.

Step Two: ...I'd have to think about it.

Maybe I'd start with the puppy and figure out some other way to get Rafe's interest after the cursed holiday season.

I glanced at the clock. Only eight. I still had time to pop down to the bodega to grab a sandwich for dinner, and then I could catch up on the episodes of *Zombified* that I'd missed.

Less than two hours from existential breakdown to healthy, normal behavior.

I was getting better at this whole faking human thing.

SUNRISE CAME WHILE I WAS CONTEMPLATING MY empty kitchen cupboards. I wasn't an early bird, but the winter sun rose around seven and I hadn't slept well. There hadn't been dreams, but emotions. A stark fear and a sudden emptiness that threatened to swallow me whole.

Well before the alarm rang, I'd kicked the covers off, showered, and dressed for a run to work. Pounding my problems into the pavement would be a good way to work off any lingering nightmares.

The lack of breakfast was a problem, though. A breakfast burrito heated up in a bodega microwave didn't sound appealing.

Neither did running.

I looked out the kitchen window to the stairs of the neighboring apartment complex. If I stood on tippy-toe and leaned forward, I could see a sliver of ocean and beach. That would work.

Ten minutes later I was on the beach in a slouchy gray sweater that had a cartoon sketch of a femme zombie and the words 'I Like Them Brainy' written across it in big, black letters. Today was ugly sweater day at the office and I was going to take my role as resident Halloween fanatic to new and frightening levels.

Or I would have, if I could have found my Jack O' Lantern Sketchers. They weren't in my closet. I didn't have a car. Which meant I'd either left them in the Charles de Gaulle airport in Paris when I'd lost my Zany Zombie tote, or they were in the corner of forgotten things in the office break room.

The beach was quiet again, and dog-free while not actually being empty. A lazy sun was climbing into the dark blue sky with all the motivation of hungover springbreakers; the ocean rolled on the shore in slow waves, not in a hurry to get anywhere. There wasn't enough Cuban coffee in the world to make the denizens of Miami Beach morning people.

I stretched out on the night-cooled sand and closed my eyes as the scent of the ocean washed over me. The beach grounded me. It was always changing but also always the same. Sand and waves moved around, but the beach—the intersection between two worlds—was unchangeable.

That was me, caught between a forgotten past and an unknowable future. Paralyzed between wanting a happier life and the feeling that I didn't deserve better. Trapped by a desire to be loved and the fear that I'd be used and thrown away again.

The rhythmic sound of a runner on the sand made me crack an eye open.

There was a jogger in the distance, rapidly closing the space between us. Black shorts. Muscular legs. Bare chest.

I wasn't ogling.

It was just hard to look away when I recognized Rafael. Part of me knew it was safer to turn, to run away and cut this short. But part of me knew that if I did, I'd be running for the rest of my life, always abandoning ship before I formed a real relationship.

"Morning," Rafe said as he came to a stop a few feet away. "Cute shirt."

"Thanks, I love yours too." I focused on his smile and not his abs. "I bet it looks great on whoever's bedroom floor you left it on."

The corners of his eyes crinkled as he laughed. "You know it's still hanging in my closet."

"Right. You'd never be that untidy."

He rolled his eyes skyward, lips pursed together, as if remembering some past romp where his shirt hadn't been hung lovingly where it wouldn't get creased. "I can't say I've ever left my clothes on a bedroom floor…"

"Living room? Car? Up on the ceiling fan maybe?"

"You've spent a lot of time thinking about where my shirt might wind up," Rafe said, taking a step forward. There was an unspoken invitation there to step forward myself. To play a little longer.

My stomach growled and I looked away.

"Skipped breakfast?"

"Nothing I had at the apartment sounded good." Brushing sand off my legs, I stood up, all too aware of the heat coming off the half-naked Rafe standing beside me, looking like he was ready for a photoshoot.

"Yeah? I know a place that does a killer breakfast platter. Huevos rancheros with an extra spicy salsa, fresh avocadoes, and this lime *creama* that's..." He did a chef's kiss into the air. "There's fresh-squeezed orange juice too."

Could I be seduced by food? Yes. Yes, I could. "How far away?"

"A couple of blocks." Rafe smiled. "We can walk together."

"Sure."

He was already turning toward the bridge across the sand dunes, and I was following.

Dragging along in his wake, really, not quite sure if it was curiosity or my stomach that I wanted to feed right now. "Are they going to let you in without a shirt on?"

Rafe's grin widened. "Trust me. I have an in with the owner."

My stomach flipped as panic overwhelmed me. "You're the chef, aren't you?" I asked as the weather-beaten wood of the bridge over the dunes creaked under our footsteps.

He looked at me, all smiles. "You'd be disappointed if I weren't."

"I fell too easily." Silly me. I shook my head. My hand tightened on the rough wooden rail of the bridge as I hesitated. If I went with him now, would the Christmas Curse ruin everything? Last night I'd struggled to think of a way to get Rafe's interest; it was hard to believe just showing up at the beach to watch the sunrise had changed anything. Real life didn't work like that.

"Too easily?" Rafe laughed, oblivious to my inner monologue. "Three years of trying to find something other than work to talk to you about and you call that easy?"

I nearly smiled. "You should have started by cooking for me."

"Would it have worked?"

"No." I shook my head. "I'm not even sure why it's working today." But I was going to let it work all the same. Blame the nightmares. Blame sleep deprivation. I didn't care. I'd gone hungry too many times to pass up free food.

The offer of friendship? That was unfamiliar. I mentally danced away from the idea, ready to test the boundaries and limits, but not to commit.

Rafe turned so he was walking backward. "I know why it's working."

"Really?"

"You have an eye for beauty and there's no way you could pass up a delicious meal with a view like this." He waggled his eyebrows and put a little wiggle into his step.

Flirt.

"Mmm, am I coming to view you or your art collection?" I tilted my head to the side as I pursed my lips. "Which really seems more plausible?"

We turned down Meridian and I scanned the fenced yards for the big, black dog.

But the only warm brown eyes I saw were Rafe's as he punched in the code to unlock his door. "Promise not to steal anything valuable?"

"You mean your art, or your heart?" I sashayed past him to stand in front of *The Storm In Her Eyes*.

Rafe closed the door and leaned on it as he kicked his sneakers off. "There's the Del we know and love. The aloof art curator who crushes men's hearts and dreams." He stepped in, close enough to kiss, but only for a moment. "Let me go shower real quick and I'll come down and make us breakfast. You can get started in the kitchen if you want."

"It is cute that you think I know how to cook anything without a microwave," I said with a teasing smile and an exaggerated southern sweet tea accent.

"You said you knew how to cook," Rafe said as he walked up the stairs backward so he could watch me.

Nude Ascending A Staircase?

No. *Tease Ascending A Staircase.*

It wasn't that he looked like a dehydrated actor with zero body fat who was starving himself to get cut abs, it was that he looked healthy, and clean, and muscular. He made me want to curl up in his arms and hide from the world. He looked like he could hear all my problems and still smile.

I looked away with a sigh.

The goal was to make Rafe fall in love with me and get a big, black dog of my own.

Looking at the expensive kitchen knives and granite countertop, I could acknowledge I was well out of my depth. Fresh-squeezed orange juice. I bet Rafe thought he was funny. There were oranges sitting in a wooden bowl on the counter, but short of physically pummeling them with my fists, I wasn't sure how to juice them.

If this was what I needed to do to make Rafe fall in love with me, I was out of the running before the race even started.

Better to admit defeat now.

There was an empty seat at a round, wooden breakfast table and an app on my phone for the local pet shelter, who were advertising a Home For The Holidays adoption schedule. I was still looking up the activity requirements for various breeds of large dogs when Rafe walked in.

Pretending I didn't notice, I kept scrolling through the webpage, watching Rafe out of the corner of my eye.

He opened a cupboard and pulled out a skillet. The cutting board was hidden in a drawer under the knives. "Huevos rancheros still sound good?"

"Mm hmm." I nodded, not daring to look up.

"I was going to mix in some of the leftover chili."

"Okay."

"Maybe dip you in chocolate later and lick you clean."

"Sure. Sounds fi—" My brain caught up with my mouth. I blinked. Licked my lips. Looked up at Rafe, who stopped to lean over me.

His eyes were sparkling. "Sure?"

"Um…" I pressed my lips together, very torn on the whole subject of being dipped in chocolate.

"I'm certain I heard you say sure."

I set my phone down. "Sure, but not tonight because I have a hot date with this phenomenal artist."

Rafe's eyes narrowed and for just a moment I saw a flash of something terrifyingly familiar. The sting of rejection was making Rafe tense up.

"Martin's gallery showing?" I reminded him, pulling the conversation back to the safe harbor of work talk.

His jaw was still tight. "You sure that's how you want to spend your night?"

"It's that or the office holiday party."

"Expensive food, fine wine, excellent conversations… or whatever Martin manages to scrounge up, because we all know he didn't hire a caterer." Rafe pulled away with a sardonic look.

"Expensive art, charming artist, and I can eat when I get home."

Rafe nodded. "True. The fridge is always stocked."

"Mine isn't," I said a second before I realized he'd invited me home after the party. My eyes widened in delighted shock. "Rafael Kane! Stop trying to spoil me."

"Why?" He laughed as he opened the fridge and pulled out eggs that he cracked into the heated pan with the confident ease of someone who had made the same meal hundreds of times. "You look good happy. You could be happy here. Why shouldn't I try to make sure you are here and happy?"

Why not indeed?

I shook my head, shying away from the game he offered. "You're moving too fast. A day ago we'd barely had a civil conversation that wasn't about a contract and now you're—"

"Inviting you to raid the fridge. I'm not proposing," Rafe said as he tossed a smile my way. The smell of chili filled the air as he warmed it next to the frying eggs. "The work party will last longer than the gallery showing anyway. Especially if Vietti is there."

I shuddered at the name. Reality settled over me like a cold front whipping across the bay. Rafe had gone from easy smiles to overt flirtation as fast as any gropey client I'd ever had.

Crossing my legs and looking at my phone, I built the barriers up between us. If I wanted casual sex, I could find it anywhere. What I wanted was something difficult to define and harder to find. Love that was passionate but nurturing, encouraging, warm. Love that would see me through the storms and wouldn't vanish as soon as the novelty had worn off.

"It's sweet of you to offer, but really, I can take care of myself. There's a good bistro on that end of town. I'll grab something there." I offered Rafe a brilliant, sunny smile.

"Okay." Rafe seemed to hesitate, his smile fading in confusion. "Well, the offer is there. Want some juice?" Somehow he'd already turned the pile of oranges into two glasses of fresh juice and the aroma of chili was perfuming the air.

"Yes, please." Now I felt guilty for not helping. "Can I do anything? Drop the orange peel in the compost? Get the plates?"

"There's silverware in the drawer." Rafe nodded to the cupboards near the fridge. "And napkins."

Feeling ridiculously invasive, I opened the drawers and got the cutlery and fabric napkins as Rafe set two plates on the table. Sure, I could walk into a stranger's house while chasing a dog, but eating was intimate. It was a ritual shared with people you cared about. The traditions were older than the city of Miami.

Rafe sat down slowly. "Is this okay?"

I took a deep breath, asking myself the same question. Slowly, I nodded. "Yeah, it's just... a little out of my comfort zone. I don't usually eat with anyone except at lunch time." And I hadn't gone on a date in years. Cut-and-run flirtations were safer, easier. This was... not easy.

"Would it help if I promised not to make this a habit?" Rafe's eyes met mine as I took a bite of the huevos rancheros.

Too late for that. The sensual taste of chili and cocoa made me groan with delight. Rafe was hot, his taste in art was exceptional, and his cooking was scandalously good. I took another bite and felt my resolve crumble.

He couldn't ghost me if I knew where he lived, right?

Rafe watched me, delight suffusing his face. "You like it?"

"You should have burnt the food. Or remembered not to feed the strays. Keep doing this and you're going to have werewolf movies in your streaming queue."

"I already have that." Rafe's eyes caught mine as he smiled. "You forgot, I'm a big fan of werewolves." He took a bite of breakfast and nodded. "It's good, isn't it?"

"It is." Half my plate was already empty. "If this art dealer thing doesn't work out, you could go into the restaurant business."

His eyes went wide with horror as he shook his head. "Weird hours. Late nights. High stress? No thank you. My sister runs a kitchen in Orlando," he said by way of explanation. "She's the lead chef Thursdays through Sunday and, I swear, one day it's going to kill her. It's too much work."

My phone rang, a familiar opera summoning me to the daily grind. "Vietti or Lisbon?" I asked as I reached for it.

Rafe looked up at the clock. "London. Someone's mad Suzanne's painting sold before auction."

"Bet you it's not."

"Loser does dishes?"

I nodded and picked up my phone. "This is Delinna from Elegant Miami," I said. As the customer spoke, I smiled at Rafe and mouthed, "Madrid."

With a groan of defeat, Rafe took my empty plate. If it hadn't been for the client talking in rapid-fire Spanish about a street artist I just had to find for him, I think Rafe would have taken more. The warmth in his chocolate brown eyes was flavored with something extra. A question and an invitation and a promise all rolled into one.

"Yes."

Rafe raised his eyebrows, stopping in the middle of the kitchen, both plates in hand.

I cleared my throat. "I mean, *si, sé quien es el artista. Te enviaré la información. Si. Si. Adios.*" I put my phone down as reality rushed in and my cheeks turned red with embarrassment. "Madrid wants me to track down a street artist from Taipei to come do a mural for them."

"How did you get that information?"

"Ran into him at a streetfest a couple years ago in Hong Kong and helped him track down a piece he wanted for his outdoor collection. But there's a twelve hour time difference and if I don't call now he'll be asleep before I can get to work. The bus—"

"Eight minutes," Rafe said. "It stops at the end of the street."

I was already mentally out the door and reviewing my basic Mandarin. There were rules and rituals and polite ways of greeting someone. Details and etiquette swirled in my mind.

It was the rituals that froze me mid-stride. Rafe had just cooked me breakfast. I should be staying to help wash dishes or ride with him to work; it was part of the ritual of eating together. But I was rushing out the door like a business customer at a café.

"Thank you for breakfast." I hesitated, but I had to do something. Shoving dread aside, I kissed Rafe's cheek before fleeing the scene of my crime.

My European customers always complain about tipping, but really, it would have been easier to drop a twenty for breakfast than to explain the kiss.

"See you at work, Del," Rafe's voice followed me as I put on my sneakers on the front stoop.

"See you soon!" I waved in the direction of the kitchen and fled down the block.

Curse my optimistic, impulsive, epicurean soul. I'd been seduced by a little attention and a very good breakfast.

Shameless. I was absolutely shameless.

But, shameless while being well-fed and in a much better mood than I'd woken up in. Maybe I'd have to start going to the beach before work more often.

PHONE CALLS TOOK UP ALL MY MORNING.

Rafe stopped by once to drop off the last of his client's paperwork for filing before the holidays, with a sticky note that had the number 3.5 written in bold and circled.

I waved him off and went back to translating a conference call in two languages that weren't my own—that I knew of. The Spanish from the client was easy enough to pick up, having lived in Miami for a decade. The Taiwanese artist, on the other hand, spoke Mandarin and German fluently. Neither of them were fluent in English.

Somehow we muddled through.

Lunch came at almost two and when my phone rang again, I almost cried. Why weren't these people asleep?

"Hello, this is Del—"

"Del!" The voice on the other end didn't have a hint of overseas accent. "Carson Vietti."

I dropped into my chair as I cursed myself for not checking my caller ID. "Mister Vietti, how can I help you this afternoon? Are all your contracts taken care of?"

One click took me to his file that listed every contract he'd signed. It looked good on my end.

"This is less of a business call than a personal one," Vietti said with an affected southern drawl. "I know you don't like the party scene and I think I may have come on a little strong the other night when I called you up."

"You were enthusiastic," I said mildly. "I'm sure the jubilance just carried you away."

"Exactly. Jubilance."

And martinis.

"So let me make it up to you," Vietti said. "I'm going out to Aspen next week. Cute little chateau up in the mountains. Skiing. Hot tubs. We can get away from everyone and catch up."

I took the phone away from my ear and stared at it, willing it to melt into slag on the spot. If I burned, so be it.

The phone didn't melt under my glare.

Hanging up probably wasn't going to work either. I forced a smile, my lips all but bleeding as they stretched into a grimace. "Mister Vietti, that's hardly necessary. Your apology is more than enough. Everyone here at Elegant Miami appreciates your enthusiasm for art. You are one of our favorite collectors. Mister Barros always sings your praises."

"Does he?" Vietti sounded intrigued.

"He does. And I could not accept being singled out. Especially since there are so many people here who have done more for you than I have."

"Barros isn't nearly as cute as you are," Vietti said in a way he probably thought was a compliment. "Let me take you out, Del. I'm sure you'd enjoy it."

My skin felt slimy just thinking about dinner alone with Vietti. "Really, I couldn't accept, Mister Vietti. It's against company policy. Oh!" I held the phone away from my face as I glared at the door. "Oh, so sorry, Mister Vietti, I need to let you go. Maureen needs me."

"Hold on a minute now. Let's talk this over."

"Really, I have to dash. Happy holidays, Mister Vietti!" I hung up as fast as I could and dropped my phone into my desk drawer, praying the battery would die.

Before anyone could get clever and try the land line, I unplugged it.

It was the holidays. I was getting off work in three hours.

Except I wouldn't be, because there were still five hours of filing left to do, and people got angry if their payments were delayed.

The office door swung open and I grabbed my scissors.

Maureen froze, face hidden behind a neon-pink Christmas tree with little mint-green flamingo ornaments. "Um, is that a no for helping me decorate for the party tonight? They aren't letting me in until five, and that's barely enough time to get the tables decorated before the food arrives."

"Do you want decorations or filing?" I asked, my stress barely leaking out into my voice.

"How about I have Chris The Secretary do the decorating and help you finish up the filing?"

"Sounds good." Maureen had many faults, but she was the fastest typist in the Miami-Dade area and she could go through files like Hollywood went through gossip.

The filing took half the time I'd expected. By a quarter after four, Maureen and I were both watching the clock and waiting to see who would break first.

Outside, a car rolled past, blasting an irreverent hip-hop holiday song about angels getting high that had been at the top of the charts all week.

That was my limit.

The hip-hop carol broke me.

If I had to spend one more minute listening to the holiday radio station playing in accounting or staring at fake snow, I was going to smash a three-thousand-dollar vase over someone's head.

But it wasn't five.

I needed an excuse. An escape hatch.

Frantically, I searched my desk, skimming the sticky notes and debris of the sales season for something, anything that would help. My eyes snagged on today's date and the words 'open house'.

In the depths of my brain, a marching band led a parade under golden fireworks as I rejoiced.

Between playing international negotiator and dodging Vietti's pathetic attempts at flirtation, I'd forgotten Martin's open house at his studio in town was tonight. It was in the same neighborhood as an animal rescue and the party started in three hours. Forty-five minutes for the bus, a few hours of playing with puppies, and then I could swing by Martin's gallery for a few minutes before the evening was over.

Flawless planning.

Except I'd gone to Rafe's house after the beach this morning instead of going home to change. Martin wouldn't care, but it was hard to get buyers to hand over millions of dollars to a girl in a sweat-shirt.

If I'd been a middle-aged white man they would have—of course—fallen over themselves to give me their money, hoodie or no.

I yanked the desk drawer where I kept my emergency clothes stash open a little harder than I meant to, sending my small tray of emergency cosmetics rolling forward. Blues popped out at me.

Frosty, shimmery blue lipstick that matched the icy blue hair of one of Martin's mermaid sculptures.

Twinkling blue folds on an expensive silk clutch one of our clients had gifted me. Hidden inside the clutch was a devastatingly simple white cocktail dress and a set of four-inch heels that could be broken apart and folded for travel.

The yoga pants, sports bra, and off-the-shoulder sweatshirt I was wearing now would fit in the clutch while I was at the party, but my cute boots wouldn't. I'd have to leave them at my desk and wear the sandals at the shelter. Not the perfect footwear for meeting new dogs, but I'd been in Miami since I could remember and I knew how to wear heels.

Maureen looked up as I wiggled in my seat, changing my footwear. "Everything all right over there?"

"No, I just remembered I need to get across town for Martin's open house tonight. If I hurry, I can catch the four thirty bus." A shade dishonest, but true enough. If Maureen checked the times, she'd realize I could review contracts for another hour. A show of reluctance would be enough to distract her.

"I thought we were skipping that."

"I was if we needed to work late, but I'm all caught up and I know Martin would really appreciate the moral support. Besides, if I have contracts in hand tonight then I have less work on Monday."

And then Tuesday was Christmas Eve. Everyone had the twenty-fourth through January second off to spend with family. Fighting back a grimace, I transferred my tiny wallet with my apartment key and phone into the clutch next to my dress.

"Well, have fun then," Maureen said, the tiniest trace of jealousy slipping into her voice.

Now for the reluctance. "Seeing *Martin* will be fun. Seeing the buyers will be... trying." No other word was suitable. Letting my bottom lip wobble, I looked to Maureen for moral support. "I spent all day on the phone with people. I don't want to deal with more people. They're so... so... people-y!"

The least she could do was acknowledge my pain.

Maureen's earrings jingled as she laughed. "Oh, sweetie, you'll be fine. You can handle anything for a few hours."

"No, not after today," I said, pretense vanishing. "Someone is going to walk in and tell me they love to take home 'fine art' and try to slip me their number."

"Oh, Martin, love the new focus of your art," Maureen said, pitching her voice an octave up and warbling with a Transatlantic accent like some starlet who retired during Hollywood's Golden Age. "How much are you, darling?" She gave me a saucy wink as Rafe and Chris The Secretary walked in.

Chris and his green hair vanished behind Rafe.

Rafe's eyes narrowed as he mouthed Maureen's words. "I always walk in at the wrong time."

"Oh, no, you're right on time," I said, too emotionally exhausted to keep my work face on. "We're taking bets on how many times someone will use the 'I like beautiful things, how much to take you home?' pick-up line on me tonight."

"A hundred says no more than twice," Maureen said. "It might be the same person twice, but once other people see how tacky it is, they'll think of something better."

Chris peeked out from behind Rafe's broad shoulders. "What are you wearing?"

"Not this."

Chris waited.

"A dress of some form, probably." Unless I spilled something on it between now and the party.

"Three," Chris said. "All men. Lesbians have better taste."

"In women or in pick-up lines?" The look I gave him sent Chris ducking behind Rafe again. "I happen to clean up rather well."

Rafe shook his head. "It won't happen."

I raised my eyebrows. "Really?"

"One look from you and everyone will keep their

mouths shut. You look ready to kill." Rafe crossed his arms.

"I'll have my office face on!" I glared at him. My acting skills were not that bad.

"Then once, and then you'll stab them with the nearest sharp object."

Far too late, I realized I was holding my scissors again. "These are to cut packing material if I need to tonight."

"You say that now." Rafe smiled to take the sting out of his words. "But those are office scissors."

With a grumble, I tossed them on the desk. See? I could be a reasonable adult. No issues. No fears. No bravado or weapons needed.

And if you believe that, I have a lost Degas painting sitting in the company safe that I'd love to sell you.[5]

Chris's green hair reappeared around Rafe's arm. "What do we get if you lose?"

"Maureen bet a hundred," I said.

She nodded. Jingle-jingle-jingle.

"A hundred is good," Rafe said.

Chris scowled at us. "I'll buy donuts if I lose. The good ones from the place in Wynwood."

---

[5] The provenance on that one was a mess. It was stolen, and then later turned out to be a forgery, but the forger was famous too and in the end the history of the painting made it more valuable than it had been initially. Barros kept it around as a conversation starter.

"I appreciate your donations to my gluttony habits and bank account," I said, shooting all three of them a dazzling smile, "because I'm winning. Rafe says zero, two for Maureen, three for Chris. Tomorrow morning, I'll be collecting from all of you."

Tossing my hair over my shoulder, I diva-walked out of the office.

In the hallway mirror, I could see Rafe watching me with a smile. It was the best thing to happen to me since breakfast.

THE BUS RIDE ACROSS TOWN WAS UNEVENTFUL, AND I arrived at the shelter well before the six o'clock closing time.

Pushing the door open, I took a deep breath of cold air, catching the lingering aromas of money, pet-safe cleanser, and chlorine.

My heels clicked on the concrete floor as I walked, echoing off walls painted with orange cartoon kittens chasing bright pink balls of string. Orange paw prints on the floor created a trail that I followed around the corner into a small waiting area with dull-gray plastic benches, an empty blue recycling bin, and a bored-looking woman chewing gum as she read a paperback with a familiar Miami Library bookmark beside it.

She was young looking, probably still in her early twenties, bleach-blonde hair striped with faded blue and green on one side. Her red shirt had a black sketch of a German Shepherd and the words 'Home for the holidays' emblazoned across it in a friendly font.

As I approached the desk, she looked up and stuck her bookmark in the book. "Hi."

"Hi." I put on a smile that said Respectable and Trustworthy. "I've come to see if you have a dog."

"Is yours missing?" the woman asked, worry flickering in her eyes.

"Oh, no. I... I was looking to adopt. Sorry."

She grimaced. "Can't help you." She looked down the hall and I followed her gaze.

The kennels were empty.

Silver-barred doors hung open and bright green stacks of feeding bowls sat stacked next to a utilitarian sink and a water hose.

"We had a big holiday push," the woman said. "The radio station came out. We had prizes and raffles. All the animals went home for the holidays, even Timothy."

"Timothy?"

"Tiny Tim the snake," she said. "He's a six-foot boa constrictor. Tiny is a joke," she explained.

I stared at the empty kennels in disappointment.

"You can come back in January," she said. "Once school is back in session we'll have a ton of surrendered pets. Everyone loves the dog until it needs attention."

"That's cynical."

"I've worked here for three years. It's the truth."

Her fingers played impatiently across the edges of her book.

There was no excuse to stay longer, but I held the feeling of disappointment a moment or two anyway. A small part of me that I didn't want to acknowledge had been hoping the big black dog was here.

I was glad he wasn't, because it meant he was probably safe and loved and happy.

But still…

Was it really that selfish to want to be the one someone was safe and loved with?

Was I really a terrible person for wanting to have company?

I tried not to overthink. Really tried not to feel like my parents had abandoned me.

And still my heart broke just a little, thinking about not seeing that dog again.

"Are you sure you weren't looking for a specific animal?" the woman asked.

"There was a big, black dog running loose the other day," I said holding my hand at hip height to indicate his size. "I tried to catch him but I couldn't. I just hope he's safe."

"He probably is. We have a city-wide lost and found pet database where we can list found animals or ones found dead on the side of the road. It means any rescue or shelter can search for a missing pet when someone comes in, but there haven't been any updates this week except the missing cat who was found this morning."

"Alive?" If I didn't ask it would keep me up all night.

She nodded and then gave me a pitying frown. "Do you want to leave a number just in case the dog shows up?"

"Yes!" I pounced on the idea. "That would be perfect."

After giving her a business card from my wallet, I went down the street to a cafe tucked into the remains of an autobody shop. Smoothies count as a dinner food in Miami. They probably count as their own food group. Frozen yogurt certainly does.

A quick drink and a quick change in the bathroom and I magically transformed from Dull Office Delinna to Sparkling, Steal-Your-Wallet Delinna who could talk billionaires into handing me stacks of cash for small pieces of art.

The owner of the cafe gave me a once over as I walked past her. "What's the special occasion?"

"Art show," I said with a contract-sealing smile. The dress was one I'd bought from a website that catered to travelers. The stretchy white fabric had an almost metallic sheen to it, was thin without being transparent, caressed my body like a lover, and—best of all—didn't wrinkle at all.

It was perfect for when I traveled because it changed with my needs.

Add a light pink lipstick and I had a garden party dress. Some gold hoops and bangles and I was ready for a day in L.A.

Tonight, the frosty blue lipstick and a large blue topaz cocktail ring turned it into mermaid chic.

I managed to make it down the block to the gallery space Martin shared with several other artists without breaking a heel or getting cat-called. It was progress.

Martin and his friends called the old building an Artisanal Commune, which sounded like a new fondue dish at a fusion restaurant on the expensive end of town. What it actually meant was that the upstairs spaces were split between studios and small apartments, with a communal kitchen and a shared gallery downstairs.

Every year, the place filled up with college drop outs in the spring and was nearly empty by late October. Hannah, the old painter who actually owned the property, spent most of her year down in the Florida Keys. The only other semi-permanent resident was going by the name Henri this year and was somewhere in Eastern Europe doing something vague and probably not legal.

Right now, Martin had the place to himself, and it showed.

The main gallery had bare walls with only a thin coat of pale, pearlescent gray stain that clashed with the extra gallery walls made of recycled wooden pallets.

Martin said he was a Trash Artist, that he took the lost and discarded things and made them beautiful. And he did. He was a genius, pulling emotion and joy out of pieces of abandoned flotsam. He turned driftwood into seductive sirens, broken bottles into jewels, trash from the beaches into art that sold for millions.

I took my time walking through the gallery, studying each piece. The star attraction sat under a spotlight directly in front of the front door, a pair of mermaids swimming close, lips almost touching, gaps in the wood filled with purple sea glass. One look and I was underwater with them.

Blushing at the vivid emotions, their unashamed looks of love.

Burning bright with a jealous anger that made me want to reach out and torch the driftwood mermaids who were loved more than I'd ever been.

"Del?" Martin sounded apologetic as he called my name.

Breathing in the air thick with the scent of briny wood, I plastered a smile on my face.

"You're early," Martin said, his voice filled with contrition. He was always like that, his tone of voice and body language begging forgiveness for encroaching on your time.

I turned and looked him over.

His family was from India three generations ago, but he was born and raised in Ohio and he spoke with a faint Midwestern accent. He had dark brown skin, beautiful black hair, and for some reason had decided his not-intolerable face would be improved by a thin mustache.

Martin's white shirt was slightly wrinkled, but paired with the black slacks his fashion-conscious mother had given him, he looked quite handsome. Except for the problematic mustache.

I sighed and shook my head, wishing away my negative thoughts. For tonight, I'd try to pretend Martin was channeling his inner… what's-his-name, the one with the wispy mustache in the historical film where he said he didn't give a damn. The actor's name escaped me. But he'd been considered very handsome almost a century ago, so I could pretend Martin was channeling his inner Golden Age Film Star.

If it got my artist through the gallery opening, I'd take it.

He sidled forward with a remorseful look. "You look quite nice tonight."

"Thank you, Martin." I beamed at him, willing some of my self-confidence into the wispy artist. "Are you all set for tonight?"

"Just about. Hannah's friend Anna brought over some food."

Panic swept over me like a summer storm. Last time Martin was in charge of the catering, he'd combined raw shrimp and mayonnaise and let it sit out for hours. Half the guests had food poisoning.

"What did you pick for the menu?" I asked as I silently prayed to any god listening that it wouldn't turn deadly. The holidays were already stomach-churningly bad.

"Crackers, mostly, and a little cheese platter and melon balls with sticks. It's all stabby food."

"Stabby food?" I followed him around the first set of backdrops to view the table and sagged with relief. He'd put a clean, Caribbean-blue tablecloth down and all the food had tiny, recyclable toothpicks. "It actually almost matches the theme of your art."

Martin's worried look vanished as he smiled. "Really? Do you think so? Did I do it right?"

"This is good, Martin. Very good." So much better than last year's debacle, but I left that unsaid.

Artists got nervous when you mentioned old failures, and it wasn't like any of us could go back in time to change the past. Though sometimes it was nice to think about what would happen if we could.

I, for instance, would like to go back a few days and keep the black dog. But thinking about that wish was useless, so I shooed the thought away.

Rubbing sweaty palms together, Martin took a deep breath and looked around. "I invited quite a few people. Everyone I know, actually. I don't know if anyone is coming though."

"We have a few minutes before it starts," I said. "Don't worry about it."

The staging of the show was eating at me.

"Martin, do you have any fabric upstairs? Maybe some old photography backgrounds or swaths left from that fashionista who ran off to Brazil? Something to cover up the wooden backdrops? I'm worried the statues will blend in with them."

"Oh!" Suddenly Martin switched from shy Ohio boy to the dazzling dragonfly of an artist that I was convinced was his true self. Hands waving in the air, he ran off muttering things in English, French, and Punjabi.

All I had to do was stand still and watch as he slapped light switches and squealed like a toddler after twelve pixie sticks.

Darkness fell over the room like a sudden afternoon storm and then the spotlights came on, embracing the sculptures with a lover's touch.

Martin giggled, and a third set of lights came on. Colored lights under each plinth illuminated the driftwood mermaids so the seaglass caught between the branches glowed.

"Oh! This is breathtaking!"

"Do you like it?" Martin asked, nervously biting at his lip and rocking from foot to foot. "Rafael came by to talk to me last week and suggested I do something with the lighting, so I made custom stands for each of the mermaids."

Rafael really had good instincts when it came to art.

"It's gorgeous, Martin. Brilliant idea." The bare backdrops were covered in velvet darkness, leaving Martin's masterpieces bathed in a magical light. Now I just needed to adjust the perimeter lighting so guests could walk around without tripping, and order a truck to take home all the cash we were going to make.

"When we open the doors, it should look like you're walking into a magical underwater grotto." Martin watched me in eager anticipation.

I nodded and circled the room, turning on the floor lighting in the places we needed it.

Martin made a startled noise.

"What?" I froze, hand halfway to a switch, caught between a spotlight and the sculpture of a brawny merman reaching toward me.

"Hold still! I need my sketchpad!"

When a nervous artist tells you to hold still, you hold still. I waited for Martin to rush to the back room and reappear.

"I have a piece of wood that looks like you," he said as he flipped open his sketchpad.

"Only you could make that sound like a compliment." I smiled because I knew he meant well.

His response was the sound of a pencil dancing across drawing paper.

Behind me I heard the doors open, bringing in a rush of warm air and two sets of footsteps, one in clicking heels and the other in heavy flats that hit the ground with an authoritative confidence.

"Oooo!" The soprano coo echoed through the gallery. "I didn't know your work extended to living sculptures, Martin. Tell me, how much to take that one home?"

Turning to the new arrivals, my gaze went straight past the woman to Rafael Kane, who was staring, eyes sweeping up my legs and widening as he smiled.

I tilted my head a little, wondering what he was thinking.

The woman walked forward, a vision of predatory femininity with white hair and a lavender suit tailored around the kind of body that made South Beach famous. "I'm Sionne." It rhymed with Dion, as in Celine. "And you are...?" She held out a lavender business card with gold metallic trim.

Business cards that matched your clothes?

That was dedication to drama.

"Del Farmer from Elegant Miami," I said with my brightest smile. "I'm here to draw up some contracts for Martin."

"Mmm." Sionne looked me up and down and then sighed happily. "Single?"

"Um...."

"Doesn't matter. I'm not the jealous type. And I adore the beautiful things in life." She made eye contact and waited.

"I love beautiful things too," I said levelly. "Have you seen the mermaid lovers statue Martin finished last month? I think you'll love the colors."

Rich people were all the same: refusal confused them, but they were easily distracted. And the statue had purple hair. It seemed like a safe bet she'd like it.

Sionne pouted. "Statuary is so distant. Are you certain I can't persuade you to consider a more personal form of art? I'm flying to Rio next week and I have room for one more. I'd make sure you were happy. Every whim catered to."

"That's a very generous offer, but my schedule is packed." My days were absolutely filled to the brim with not being with Sionne. Or Vietti.

Or anyone.

She sighed in defeat. "Very well, Martin, let me see the mermaids. Del, keep my card in case you change your mind."

"I will."

I would, too. It would get a place in my Problematic People folder, next to Vietti and half of the Miami 1%.

Martin led her to the far side of the gallery and I hit a mental reset button.

People with too much money thought everything was for sale. I was used to it. And, all in all, Sionne was polite about it.

Rafe caught my eye and raised an eyebrow. He'd traded in his white button down for a tight, black shirt and dark jeans that hugged his sculpted body like a second skin. The outfit was similar to the one he'd worn in a modeling campaign the same winter I was living on the street.

And he'd walked in with Sionne. Ouch. If he was going to batter my pride like that, the least he could do was pay up. Smiling, I sauntered over to him. "You lost the bet. I can't murder a poor, old lady."

"She's not even sixty," Rafe said with an amused scoff. "And she's rich. Her family did well in the green energy push a decade ago."

"Lucky her." I looked around the room again, assuring myself everything was in place for maximum profit, and caught Rafe eyeing my thighs. I snapped my fingers by my hip.

His gaze flew up to my face with an unrepentant smile. "I'm going to lose that bet, aren't I?"

"You are." I smiled back and let him get an eyeful. Rafe could go chase the Lady in Purple if he wanted, but I was too competitive to give up without a fight.

There was a hunger in his look, a predator's confidence as he closed the space between us, a heat that begged to be followed by a touch. Rafe stopped a few torturous inches away. The heat settled in his eyes and his gaze caressed me.

I tilted my head, feigning a confidence that was only skin deep. "Like the dress?"

"Love it. Where'd you find it?" He frowned a little as he craned his neck to look at my back and legs.

"Something wrong?"

"I'm looking for the foundation lines."

I repeated the statement in my head twice and still my brain was blinking 'Error 404 – Data Not Found'.

"What?"

"Your spanx. That dress looks so thin, but I can't see a single line from your foundation garments. I know a couple of models who would kill to know what brand you're wearing."

"I'm not wearing any at all. It's an eighty dollar dress from a travel website and the only thing hidden under it is me."

He whispered something under his breath in Spanish that sounded like a prayer but was probably a curse.

Whichever it was, it made me want more. The look in Rafe's eyes made me feel powerful in a way Vietti's smarmy smile never could. Like touching a fire and being able to hold the flames instead of being burnt. I knew it was dangerous, but I wanted to play anyway. I stepped closer to him, testing the limits— his and mine. "I run on the beach a lot. I eat well enough, even if it's bodega lunches and food trucks. This is all natural."

"Suddenly I have an urge to eat organic." His grin was delightfully wicked as he touched the small of my back and pulled me in.

I smiled back. There was the Rafe I'd been playing with this morning. The one I wanted to play with every day but was scared to hold on to. "Focus on the artwork, Rafe."

For a half-second it looked like he was going to make a clever remark about me being the art, but he caught himself. With a rueful grin, Rafe looked away, surveying Martin's work. "What was Martin sketching when we walked in?"

"Don't know." I had the urge to lean my head against his chest for a moment. The stress of the day, of Vietti's unwanted attention, the disappointment of not finding my dog—all of it could be washed away as I listened to Rafe's heartbeat. I wanted it, but I couldn't force myself to make the next move. "He told me to freeze and that he had a piece of wood shaped like me."

"That's a compliment, coming from Martin."

"I know." A lavender monster walked past us with an angry pout. "So... breakfast with me and dinner with Sionne? That seems..."

"Wrong?" Rafe suggested with a chuckle. "Sionne is strictly a client. I went to the company party for a bit and then swung by here to check on Martin."

"The hot date is waiting for you somewhere else?"

His hand slid to my hip, polite, but definitely testing the waters. "Oh, yeah. At home, hot and wet. There's candles." Hunger flickered in his eyes as the corner of his lips curved up into a delicious smile. "But the bubble bath can wait."

I laughed, covering my mouth. "A bubble bath?"

"Yes, a bubble bath," Rafe said, grinning as he stepped away. "What were you thinking?"

"Oh... I..."

He tsked. "You're picking up bad habits from Maureen."

"Pretty sure my bad habits came pre-equipped." I tried not to let my gaze linger on Rafe's tight, black shirt. It was a losing battle.

Rafe turned, flexing an arm and posing. "What are you thinking about now?"

"Photography."

"Photography and bubble baths?" He raised an eyebrow. "That wasn't the kind of art I expected you to like."

Unbidden, the picture of a playful Rafe sitting in a hip bath covered by bubbles came to mind. It would the perfect black and white image for the tastefully decorated washroom of someone with a cheeky sense of humor, Rafe blowing a pile of bubbles at the viewer like a he was blowing a kiss.

I knew the perfect frame for it too.

Rafe stepped closer. "Where is your mind at, Miss Farmer? Because that smile playing on your lips makes me want to come play with you."

I pulled my gaze from his muscular chest to his chocolate brown eyes as my grin widened. "Just picturing a photo shoot."

"Oh?" He leaned closer.

"A very tasteful photo shoot." Even if the thought of it made me weak at the knees.

"Really?" Another inch and our lips would touch.

"You were wearing mostly bubbles." My move, and we were centimeters apart, caught in a moment like the two mermaids, so close and yet so far away. I wanted to close the space—to answer the siren's call in his eyes—and I was afraid I would drown there.

"And what were you wearing in this fantasy?" Rafe's voice was a whisper against my skin.

"Nothing?" The fantasy only had him. I blinked. The magical moment popped like a soap bubble and my brain caught up with my mouth too late. "I mean, I wasn't in the fantasy. I was thinking of a photo. After the fact. Black and white."

Rafe shook his head, his smile gentle. "You stopped making sense."

"Where'd I lose you?"

He grinned impishly. "At the part where you weren't playing in the bubbles with me. Are you certain there wasn't chocolate involved?"

My cheeks burned in delighted embarrassment. I was lucky the lights were low or someone would have thought Rudolph's red-cheeked sister had broken into the gallery. "It was not that kind of thought." I cleared my throat and refocused, pulling away from him just a little. "Why are you here, actually? I thought you were going to skip this."

"I was, but then we had the bet and Maureen said your new puppy would be here."

I deflated slightly. "The shelter already adopted all the pets out." My mood shifted. "And they hadn't seen my black dog."

"Your black dog?" Rafe sounded amused.

"You know, the wolfy one."

"The monster who broke my screen door? You want him?"

I gave Rafe my best glare, which was nowhere near as effective as his sexy smile. "I happen to like werewolves."

"Oh, yeah, that's what all the women say. Right until the dog starts shedding. What happens when you have black fur all over this very exquisitely distracting dress?"

"Then I take the dress off and wash it."

There was a speculative gleam in his eyes as his lips curved into a devilish grin. "We need to get you a dog."

"Now you agree?" Ridiculous man.

"Oh, yes. You can take that dress and leave it with my shirt that was missing this morning." He winked at me.

"Rafe!"

"Del!" Martin shouted, interrupting my pleasant flirtation.

I turned to see my anxious artist waving his hands wildly, about to knock over some million-dollar mermaids.

Rafe made a disgruntled noise. "I guess this means I can't steal you away."

"No. No art theft for you tonight."

He chuckled.

"You lost the bet, by the way."

"I know. How about I pay you back at dinner tomorrow night?"

I nodded. "That sounds good. I'll see you then."

"You know where I'm at if you want to see me sooner." Closing the distance between us, Rafe brushed each cheek with the hint of a kiss. "Goodnight."

I'd get a dozen or more air kisses tonight. Rafe's would be the only ones I enjoyed.

"Del!" Martin waved frantically.

Too quickly, I was pulled into the crowd of Martin's admirers and collectors.

The last I saw of Rafe was a wave in the distance as he left.

By the time Martin's show ended, the buses were done running for the night. Taking a cab would cut into my after-holiday shopping spree budget, and walking home would clear my head.

For the record, a grand total of six people had compared me to the art work and asked if I was for sale. And I killed none of them.

There had to be a way to leverage that into a holiday bonus.

Despite the season, and the unquestionable chill in the air, I felt almost buoyant. A little floaty.

Martin had sold nearly every piece in his collection. My commissions off the sales were enough to fund a much-needed tropical get away come February. Australia sounded nice this time of year. Sydney had an amazing art scene.

There were a bunch of happy thoughts to distract myself from the memory of Rafael Kane holding me in his arms. I didn't have to deal with the possibilities of heartbreak if I didn't acknowledge what I was feeling... Right?

At the art show, we'd been in a magical mermaid grotto filled with dreams, captured for a moment by Martin's skill. But that was all it was. A moment. A single, enchanting, intoxicating, elusive moment.

Dinner and breakfast? Anomalies.

The kiss before work? A social nicety. Completely normal in artistic circles.

Rafe's kiss at the art show? A tiny flirtation.

It wasn't serious. We weren't sharing secrets or calling each other in the middle of the night just to talk. I didn't want to read too much into his attention.

Right now I was tired, and empty. Almost light-headed. It was like my emotions had washed away with the touch of night, putting me to sleep. I was waiting for something to wake me up.

At 10th Street, I turned east and followed the smell of the sea breeze past the park to the beach. I glanced back once, thinking I'd heard footsteps, but the street behind me was empty, and the beach in front was beckoning. The sand was easier on my feet and I preferred the sound of the ocean to the cheerful drunkenness of the tourists spilling out of the bars on Ocean Drive, the ocean brine to the smell of car exhaust.

There were strands of colored lights adorning the balconies of the apartments overlooking the beach.

I wasn't feeling angry about the lights.

I wasn't feeling cheated.

After eleven years, if I closed my eyes, I could picture a family. The father looked like Mr. Barros, with his thick hair dyed black to hide gray, a Cuban accent spilling from his lips when he talked too fast or was tired. Maureen was either the strange aunt or the curious mother; either way she was the nosy, intrusive, trustworthy mamma hen in my life. Martin was like the little brother I'd probably never had, enthusiastic about everything but always anxiously awaiting approval.

And Rafe?

Rafe with his flirty breakfasts and warm smiles? I could picture curling up next to him in any cozy holiday scene ever painted.

I checked my phone, wondering if it was too late to call.

No. The battery was at three percent, and it was two in the morning. I yawned at the thought. At least I didn't have to be up early tomorrow. I could lie in bed, sleep until noon, get a late lunch, and still have time for laundry before dinner with Rafe tomorrow.

Headlights from a car spotlighted me for a second, shattering my waking sleep.

Friendly beach or no, there were rules to survival in Miami, and one of them was Always Be Careful Of Strange Cars. Could be a lost tourist. Could be a drunk. Could be a normal Miami driver. Could be a serial killer.

If you treated every car slowly crawling along Ocean Drive after midnight like a serial killer, you didn't get serial killed. Or hit by lost and drunk tourists.

I took a turn past the park and the apartments, walking on the narrow sidewalk meant for residents, hurrying between buildings until the street was quiet again.

Close to 6th, I turned back to Ocean Drive and heard voices.

"It's not a bad job. He just wants an address." In the humid night air, the voice carried. It sounded familiar.

Despite the brain trauma, I had a good memory for names and faces. It was a requirement for anyone selling to the rich, who expected everyone to love and adore them. Admitting that you couldn't keep your socialites straight was liking begging to be snubbed from the next charity gala.

"Weird request is all," a second voice said against the scuff of rubber-soled shoes on the cement sidewalk.

Both were deep, masculine, with the kind of accent people picked up from watching too many movies. The fake Jersey accent.

"The guy handed us cash," the first one said as their footsteps echoed in the quiet night. The way he pronounced *cash* was the clue. Craig, the meaty muscle-head who had a gym addiction and worked as a bouncer for some of the nicer clubs when his main boss was out of town.

"Cash is good," the second one said.

I didn't know his voice, but I knew his type, the wannabe who was clinging to Craig, hoping to pick up muscle work for someone important.

What they were doing in my part of town afterhours was none of my business. It could be anything from looking up a corner store that sold

mango Fantas to visiting someone's business part-
ner. Whatever it was, I was—in the words of a Miami
police detective I'd crossed paths with more than
once—the worst witness in the world.

Better if I saw nothing, really, because if I saw
something, it couldn't be used in court. Any defense
attorney worth their nine-hundred-dollar shoes
would use my teenage memory loss to poke holes in
my testimony.

Besides, it wasn't a bad night for a walk on the
beach, and the random car had likely gone by now. It
wasn't fear as much as it was common sense.

Quietly, I skirted around the voices and back to
the beach.

The waves lapped against the shore in the de-
ceptively calm way they did before a storm, like they
were resting. In a day or two they'd rage, chewing
through the shore to try and break the dunes.

A ghost-white crab scuttled from one hole to
another, oblivious to my presence.

Somewhere I heard the lyrics to Miami's favorite
carol. "Angels gettin' high, alright."

I hummed along as I took the bridge across the
dunes. This was a quiet area after hours. The beach
was closed at night, the bars were several blocks
away, and homeless shelter had rooms to spare since
the city implemented the Houses For All initiative
last year. At most, there might be a few hopeful
stargazers, maybe someone coming home from a late
shift.

The bright headlights of a car blinded me as it turned. Someone cursed.

My phone rang, a stabbing sonata in the darkness. I silenced it as fast I could fumble for the screen, my heart racing.

Coincidence.

All of this was coincidence.

It was just a car, not a big deal. There was no reason for anyone to be looking for me. No reason for anyone in Miami to call at 2 a.m., either.

What time zones were Lisbon and Hong Kong in and did no one there respect weekends? Grumbling, I looked at my screen.

One missed call... *Carson Vietti.*

Barros might flatter big clients, but getting employee information out of him was harder than getting access to a stranger's bank account in the Cayman Islands. My boss knew what kind of monsters we played with. He knew how to protect his employees.

But Vietti knew I walked from work. He was probably at the company party—clients were always invited to drop in at our social events. From there it wouldn't be hard to find out where I was or where Martin's gallery was. Someone in sales would be eager enough to share the information if it meant a commission.

Unrelated incidents I'd dismissed fell into a line, an unbroken chain of intention and expectation, a pattern I'd ignored.

My phone vibrated again. I turned it off.

Vietti, the handsy, drunken, aging Miami playboy who was used to people tripping over themselves to please him... Would he really send someone to find my address just because I'd refused to meet him at a club?

Yes.

My stomach churned as the muscles in my shoulders knotted with worry.

Vietti might not be willing to wait for me outside, but he would be more than happy to pay Craig and his buddy to wait nearby and follow me home. Once he had my home address, it would only be a matter of time before he showed up at my door.

The local police department already had their hands full. "My client is planning to stalk me" was not going to get any traction. I'd have to wait for Vietti to actually hurt me or threaten me in some measurable way.

I didn't want to be hurt. I wanted to be safe.

If I'd sprung for the expensive condo with a front lobby and good security, I could have run in screaming. In my dress and heels, that would have been enough to get everyone's attention.

But my apartment was in a narrow building squished between hotels. It was all that was left of some premium condos after a hurricane several years ago. Half the building had been destroyed, so the owners sold to the hotel, who used it primarily as cheap, local housing for the staff. The rooms that weren't rented out at a discount to the hotel bartenders, masseuses, and cleaning staff were available to other locals. The kind of people who got ignored when they screamed.

Coming off the beach, I could see past the deserted courtyard, where a collection of doomed palm trees waited to die of neglect, to the main street. The car from the beach had parked on the street right nearby.

There were large, iron gates on two sides of the courtyard, and a ten-foot-tall cement wall painted white on the other.

A scuff on the pavement drew my attention. Craig. He'd positioned himself so he could see the hotel lobby and the main apartment entrance. His friend was on the other corner, watching the hotel service entrance and the back gate.

That left me with... Scaling the wall? Going to another apartment? Going to a hotel for the night?

Going to Rafe?

I wiped sweaty palms along the skirt of my dress as I mulled over my options. I could go back to the beach, circle around, and sneak down to Rafe's house.

Would he want to see me at three in the morning?

More to the point, could I handle seeing Rafe when I was tired, scared, and panicky?

Probably not.

The hotels weren't a bad option, but there was no guarantee anyone had a vacancy and no promise the lobby staff hadn't also been paid by Vietti, who might suspect I'd try that if I caught wind of his plan. All I needed was for one eager helper to accept ten thousand cash and I'd wake up with Vietti in my room.

Not an exaggeration. I had it happen one time when I was in college.

I got drunk at a friend's party and decided to stay at the venue rather than drive home to the dorm. The only thing that saved me was that I was drunk, but not black-out-and-forget-things drunk. I was in the shower behind a locked door with a cellphone when the guy came into my hotel room. I'd talked to the police wrapped in a cheap hotel bathrobe with mascara streaked down my face as the guy explained it was an honest mistake.

My word versus his.

So fun.

I did not need a repeat.

Leaning against the cold cement wall, I took off my shoes and broke them down, pulled my leggings and bra from my clutch, and did one of those impressive quick changes that one picks up being part of a theater troupe for a semester after college. I'd played Beatrice in a remake of *Much Ado About Nothing*—possibly the worst Beatrice ever to grace a Miami stage. I'd still been the best actor in that troupe though.

Stuffing the little white dress into my clutch, I looked up at the wall.

Ten feet. A little over three meters.

Not an impossible climb for someone who practices parkour or free running.

A little bit harder for someone who hadn't done anything like parkour since the last time she lived on the street. There was no handy shed, air conditioning unit, stack of trash cans, or other make-shift climbing apparatus—for obvious reasons. If I—a mostly law-abiding art contracts minion—could see a way to break into the apartments, so could every other nefarious cretin lurking on the streets of Miami Beach.

Which meant, like, three teenagers and one octogenarian cat burglar who sometimes wandered away from the retirement home on West Avenue. Miami Beach is much more into white collar crime and drug dealing.

I took a few steps back, ran, and jumped, trying to grab the top of the wall.

I got high enough to high-five an NBA point guard, but not close to the top.

I tried again and bruised my knees.

The sound was enough to attract Craig.

Crouching down low, I snuck around the far corner. My breathing sounding too loud in the night.

Craig's friend was staring at his phone screen, ruining his night vision. Perfect for me. But unless he had earbuds in, he was going to hear me opening the gate.

Maybe I could sleep on the beach. I ran a hand across my cold arm, shivering.

A scratching, scuffing sound on the sidewalk made me duck in fear. There was nothing there, only shadows cast by moonlight and streetlamps. I pressed my back against the wall.

Could have been a mouse, or a lizard, or—

Craig screamed.

His friend looked up from the phone and ran away from the corner, leaving the apartment gate clear.

Rushing to my feet, I sprinted to the gate, typing in my code as fast as my fingers would move.

The gate lock box thought for a painfully long moment as my heart hammered in my chest. With a drowsy sort of reluctance, the light turned green.

I pulled the gate open as something dark rushed around the corner.

"Something knocked me down!" Craig yelled into the night. "Big monster!"

There was a very canine sort of whine.

Peering into the shadows around the courtyard, I found a darker patch of night and a pair of glowing eyes. "Hello, puppy," I whispered. "Do you want to go out?" I held the gate open.

The dog walked into the clump of hibiscus bushes that lined the brick pathway to the stairs.

"Guess not." I pulled the gate closed behind me and crept up the stairs, lurking in the shadows and peering around pillars until I made it to the questionable safety of the third floor. It wasn't until I was inside, the door locked and the curtains closed, that my hands stopped shaking. Focusing on calming my breathing, I pulled out the emergency candle I had for hurricane season and showered in the candlelit darkness, not daring to turn the lights on.

Vietti's hunt would be a wild goose chase. Tomorrow, Craig would report that I hadn't been seen on this end of town. On Monday, I'd have a quiet word with Barros. This would all be over in the next forty-eight hours. I was fine.

As I climbed into bed, I considered turning my phone on to text Rafe and let him know I was home safe and sound—but that could wait. I'd tell him about this at dinner tomorrow, when I was calmer. What he didn't know wouldn't hurt him.

IT WAS PAST TEN IN THE MORNING WHEN I WAS AWAKE enough to realize the bananas on my counter were too green to eat and I'd forgotten to bring home anything edible from Martin's party. Grumbling, I tucked a bookmark into a fading paperback copy of *The Wolves Of Addison County* and pulled on a breezy beach dress, which was the most clothes I felt the need to wear when on holiday. A pair of flipflops, my tiny canvas purse hanging off a band of knotted five-fifty cord, and my sunglasses, and I was good to go.

Sighing and squinting at the bright sunshine as I opened the door, I stepped out—and nearly tripped as I tried to avoid the big, black dog snoring on my stoop. Somehow I managed to stay upright, not step on the dog, and not break my ankle, which was a significant accomplishment, all things considered.

The dog whined and looked up at me.

"Sorry, did I interrupt your beauty sleep?"

He smiled up at me with doggish enthusiasm.

"Why are you here?" I asked, as if the dog was going to answer me. "You should be at home."

The black dog wagged his wolfy tail.

I sighed. No collar. No tags. No leash. If I shooed him away he'd probably get hit by a car. I pushed my door open and nudged the dog in.

He whined.

"It's just for a minute. I need to find something leash-y. I can walk you into town and see if anyone is looking for you. Let you pee at least." Unless he'd done that already. The doorway didn't smell like dog though, so he'd probably been a good boy.

I could head down to the shop on Meridian and 6th. If the dog spotted his house on the way there, so much the better. All I needed was something to make it look like I was a dog owner, and not engaged in aiding and abetting a runaway Good Boy.

The dog sat patiently in the middle of my living space, looking around the room with the same critical eye I'd expect out of someone at work.

"No judging," I told the dog as I pulled the curtain back on my DIY closet space. "I didn't have much to work with."

A belt? No, too short. And I didn't want to choke the dog.

A scarf? Maybe an infinity scarf for the collar and a long scarf tied to the infinity scarf?

I glanced at the dog. Big. Black. Cheerful. "You shouldn't be this hard to accessorize."

One furry ear lifted up in canine confusion.

"It's Miami. You need to look good even if you're a tourist dog. Look at me? Effortlessly elegant and all I did was pull on an over-sized shirt dress. Sort of."

The dog padded toward me and sniffed at the dress.

"It's elegant enough to hit the corner store in on a holiday weekend. I'm not going to a party." Although I *had* worn the dress to beach parties before.

I pulled out my scarf collection and decided on an ombre effect. A deep, ocean blue infinity scarf with a two consecutively paler scarves for the leash. The lightest colored scarf faded to almost white on one end because of The Incident With The Bleach and it blended well enough with the cream fabric of my dress to be a convincing style choice. When I leaned over to secure the scarf-leash, the dog licked my face.

"I love you too. Now," I stood up and opened the door, "let's go find your humans. Or breakfast. Whichever comes first."

I locked the door behind us and paraded downstairs as if nothing were wrong. Sneaking around with pets made landlords look at you and check your lease for pet fees. Swanking through the courtyard as if the pet was already paid for made the landlords look the other way.

But it didn't matter, none of my neighbors were around anyway. They'd probably gone somewhere cold enough to shiver for winter.

Why anyone wanted to be cold was beyond me, but there were people who thought winter holidays weren't real holidays unless they were risking frost-bite.

Out of habit, I turned on 5th, taking my usual route to the shops. At the corner of Meridian and 5th, the dog sat down.

I looked at him.

He looked at me.

"Too tired to walk?" I asked without sympathy. "Too bad. I'm not carrying you. Come on." I gave the scarves a little tug, trying to convince the dog to turn north toward 6th street and brunch.

The dog bowed his head, and the scarf slipped over his ears and onto his muzzle. His ears perked up in an expression of canine confusion.

"It's a scarf, not a proper leash," I explained, tugging the scarf back down around his neck. "Come on, brunch buddy, let's go find food. You like food." He had to. Dogs loved food. Everyone knew that. It was in every dog food commercial.

Muttering encouragement to the dog, I stepped into the crosswalk. The scarf went tight for a heartbeat, then slack again as the dog stood.

I was halfway across the street before he bolted away, blue scarves flying behind him like a banner behind an advertising plane. "Wait!"

Too late. He was already dashing down the street, crashing through the bushes, and blitzing through the yards like the discount version of Santa's reindeer. I followed as fast as flipflops would allow and found myself staring at the familiar surroundings of Rafe's house.

The trio of scarves lay accusingly in the driveway under the shade of an oak tree. Spanish moss hanging off the branches swayed in the ocean breeze as I listened for the sound of a dog, or the slam of a door.

A black-and-yellow bananaquit trilled angrily at me from the branches.

Everyone's a critic.

My stomach rumbled, reminding me that my last real meal was a smoothie over twelve hours ago.

The dog had gone. I sniffed and tried not to feel a little betrayed. Clearly the dog was well-loved and had a home. I wasn't trying to steal it or anything. I just wanted company.

Okay, maybe I'd considered not looking to see if the dog was microchipped for a day or two. Or secretly hoped I'd run into the owner so I could volunteer to dogsit on occasion. But, whatever.

It was the holidays.

Holidays were made for being abandoned.

I marched up the drive, snatched my scarves off the sidewalk and looked around Rafe's backyard. How he'd managed to find a lot with an actual backyard was beyond me, even if it was a small space tucked in between apartments and another small house. Old oaks, heavy with Spanish moss, took up most of the yard, with hibiscus shrubs competing for the remaining space. A laundry line had been stretched along the back of the driveway and had jeans and t-shirts hanging in the sun. There was an old, brown truck with a dented sideboard and a pair of denim-clad legs sticking out from underneath.

I stepped back quietly.

Last night I'd looked fantastic. Now I looked exactly like someone who'd woken at every little sound and needed a shower.

Hopefully Rafe would stay busy with the truck and ignore me.

The dog was nowhere in sight.

As I turned to leave, I heard a rustling near the battered wooden privacy fence between Rafe's house and his neighbors, and a little yip.

Frowning, I walked over to where the fence was hidden by a row of scraggly shrubbery. Peering through the gap in the wood, I saw a well-cared for lawn and several dogs romping. A small yellow Lab, an even smaller Dachshund, two mutts speckled white, brown, and black—and, at the far end of the yard, a wolfy black tail hanging out of a wooden dog house.

"What are we looking at?"

I froze at Rafe's whisper in my ear. I hadn't heard a thing.

"Is that your dog?"

"It's probably the one I was chasing." I sighed and turned, running straight into shirtless abs. "Oh!" My hand traced a path down Rafe's bare chest. "Abs of treason. Wow." He'd looked good at a distance. Touching him was…

I pulled myself away, bumping into the fence.

"Here, let me help, you've got kudzu tangling around your legs." Rafe's hands were large and warm as they settled on my waist and lifted me out of the shrubs.

I landed inches from him, my back to the house, and his arms settled around my waist. Licking my lips, I tried to stop the storm of thoughts rushing through my mind. Now was not the time to think about the dog, or last night, or happy futures—but, in the eye of the storm, all I could see was Rafe's smile.

"Good morning." The look in his eye made me want to melt into him.

"Good morning." I smiled back, letting my hands slide up his chest and twine around his neck. "Surprise?"

Rafe leaned down, close enough to kiss. "I like this kind of morning surprise. I was beginning to worry Sionne had convinced you to run away with her when I didn't hear from you last night."

"I got in late," I explained. "And my battery was low. Forgive me?"

Rafe's arms tightened a little, pulling me closer. "Of course."

My cheeks burned. I was used to aggressive, demanding flirtation from people like Vietti and Sionne who saw me as another underling for sale.

Rafe's attention was different. Direct, but not demanding. Present, but not overwhelming.

I was still trying to think of a witty reply when my stomach rumbled. "Right, I need to go get breakfast. Brunch. Whatever meal of the day it is." Reluctantly, I pulled away.

Rafe caught my hand. "Wait, I happen to know a great brunch place near here." There was a flirtatious sparkle in his eyes that was infectious.

I smiled up at him, fighting the urge to close the gap between us. "Really? Does it allow you arrive shirtless and barefoot?"

He widened his gorgeous brown eyes in dramatic shock. "As a matter of fact, it does allow you to dine shirtless!"

"Really?" I played along, exaggerating my surprise. "It isn't called Rafe's Kitchen, is it?"

"It is!"

That sounded perfect. But... "We're having dinner tonight."

"Is there a rule you can't eat two meals in a row together?"

There was a very good argument against this behavior and all I could think about was the bronze ripple of Rafe's abs. *Woof.* I could picture licking chocolate off those abs.

I covered my eyes.

"Problems?" Rafe was laughing at me.

"Nope. None at all. Especially if you have chocolate." Oh. Wait. I didn't mean to say that out loud. The burn in my cheeks spread down my neck. I was going to look like a sunburned tourist if I didn't get out of here.

A dry leaf crunched under Rafe's foot as he stepped closer. "Do you like *dark* chocolate?"

It was the spin of the word that undid me, the tone and drawl. "Rafe!" I dropped my hand to glare at him properly. "Would you please stop being so ridiculously good looking so I can go get things done?"

He looked skyward as if he were pretending to consider it. "Mmmm. No." His eyes were dark and hungry as he looked back at me. "This feels like fair play after last night."

I took several very sensible steps backward, bumping into the wooden steps at his back door. "Last night?"

"That was a very, very distracting dress you were barely wearing."

My smile turned to a smirk. "It was perfectly appropriate for the venue."

"Mmm." Rafe stopped short of the stairs and fell toward me, hands catching on the rails beside me so I was trapped between him and the house.

I tossed my hair and smiled, refusing to be intimidated. Loving the attention.

The way Rafe looked at me made me feel like the

center of the universe. His smile made me beautiful. "You had me worried last night. The way everyone was looking at you, I thought you might be half way to Hawaii before our date tonight."

"Date?" I blinked in surprise. "Did we say date? I thought it was just dinner between friends. Just you paying off a bet."

"Was a bet," Rafe said, looking like he might take a bite of me just for the fun of it. "Could be a date, if you're interested. Turn our casual flirting into something a little more official."

There was a hook of a question in his words. An underlying vulnerability, as if he thought I might reject him. This wasn't Rafe teasing me because it was a Saturday morning and he had nothing better to do.

He was serious.

A cool ocean breeze blew between us. "Do you do office romances?"

"Not usually, but everyone else in the office is in a relationship."

"So it was a lack of opportunity, not a lack of interest?"

"It was both," Rafe said. "Because I didn't think you were interested in me or an office romance."

"Ah, well, confusion on both sides then." I took another step up to the door.

Rafe followed, a hungry wolf tracking his prey.

Old fears bubbled up. Loss. Rejection. Abandonment. "There are so many ways this could go wrong."

"There are so many ways this could go right," Rafe countered. "Horror movies. Chocolate. Bubbles…"

I narrowed my eyes.

"You wouldn't say no to gourmet pizza ordered in and a *Timberwolf Town* marathon on my couch, would you?" Rafe's smile grew more confident.

With a gasp of mock outrage, I said, "Using my love of werewolves against me? That's cheating!" And smart. What was it about smart men that made them so darn sexy?

Hands behind my back on the doorknob, I leaned toward Rafe until we were nose to nose. Making eye contact, I closed the gap and kissed him, barely touching my lips to his before jumping out of reach and ducking through the screen door.

This time I remembered to leave my shoes on the porch.

Rafe ran up the stairs barefoot and came through the door like a hurricane, lifting me off my feet and spinning me around. He set me on the kitchen table, which was low enough that we were eye to eye.

My heart raced in anticipation.

Grinning, Rafe closed the space between us. His lips were soft and warm, generous and inquisitive. His tongue slipped past my lips, dipping in for a taste before darting away again. He bit gently at my lip, nibbled at my neck.

Time stopped as I pulled his face back to mine. I wanted everything. His time. His touch. His kisses. His laughter.

I was greedy for every sensation, for the way he made me feel like I was floating.

I was hungry... Actually hungry. My stomach rumbled and Rafe stopped kissing me long enough to look me in the eyes.

"Should I feed you?" The pulse in his neck was racing too.

"Maybe? I don't want you to stop holding me." That won me another kiss that started at my lips and traced its way down my neck to the neckline of my dress.

Rafe growled in frustration. He broke away, stepping back and putting his hands on his hips. "This is a problem."

"No it's not."

"You need to eat. And I need to get that truck to my brother." He took a deep breath and licked his lips as his gaze wandered across my body. "I don't suppose you want to go for a drive this afternoon?"

Old fears strangled my joy. "I... don't do cars around the holidays." It was habit as much as superstition. "Besides, don't we have to exchange some deep, dark secrets or something before we meet the family?"

Rafe's smile turned to a pouting grimace as he reluctantly let go and turned to the fridge. "What's there to tell? I know you're an orphan. You have no memory of your life before that winter when you were seventeen. You don't like cars, Christmas, or cubist paintings. You love all things Halloween, werewolves, and me." He smiled brightly as he cracked eggs into a dish.

Hopping off the table, I sauntered over to the kitchen island, taking a seat on one of the padded bar stools. "And what are your deep, dark secrets?"

"Ooo, that's harder." Rafe winked as he smiled at me. "Let's see. We all know I'm bi, gorgeous, and absolutely monogamous. I have excellent taste in fashion, lovers, food, and art. So no big surprises there. Mmm, I guess the only thing people might not guess is that I watch every show about teenage werewolves and think, 'I can relate.' Big werewolf fan."

"That's it? That's your deep dark secret?" I asked as he pulled potatoes from the freezer. "You've got to give me more than that."

"Sometimes I get hairy on the weekends." He dragged a hand across his smooth jawline. "I don't always shave."

My imagination skipped away to play with that idea. The haunting image of Rafe with a five o'clock shadow and no shirt. The rough friction of stubble as he kissed me. The tickle as he kissed my neck and went lower. I bit my lip.

"Del?"

"Hmm?" Rafe was standing close, a smile on his face. A wicked, knowing smile that grew wider the longer I looked at him. "That was quite a face journey you just went on."

"Oh." My face flushed.

"I felt a little voyeuristic sitting here watching you nibble on your lip," his voice was smooth and low. Seduction and temptation in one delicious package.

I licked my lips and Rafe's eyes tracked my tongue like his life depended on it. "I have a very good imagination."

"Oh?" His gaze met mine, the eye-sex equivalent of pinning me to a wall. "Did you decide you're okay with me being hairy on the weekends?"

"Oh, yes." Hot Miami nights, Rafe wasn't even touching me and I was about to combust.

And Rafe was grinning like he knew it. He covered his mouth with his hand, the look in his eyes enough to keep me mesmerized for a lifetime. "So..."

"So?" Time for a new topic? Yes, please, because I was physically incapable of getting out of this conversation with my dignity intact.

"Should I ask you what kind of wedding you had planned?"

Not where I thought we were going with this. I blinked at him, wide-eyed and confused. "Wedding?"

"You're going to make an honest man out of me. Aren't you?" Rafe winked.

"Well..." Fine, we were going to joke and tease and pretend I was not seriously considering stripping his jeans off here in his kitchen. "You know I had that wedding magazine, and it's full of useful tips."

"Oh?"

"And one of the number tips for brides is that you

shouldn't start dating and get married in the same year. Very gauche."

Rafe's eyes narrowed slightly and then flicked to the calendar on the wall. "I don't think I've ever been happier to see New Year's Eve on the horizon."

I laughed because he wasn't serious, despite the hungry look in his eyes. "Dating this week, engaged next week, married by Valentine's?"

"Sounds perfect to me." Rafe plated the scramble of beans, sweet peppers, eggs, and potatoes with a thick layer of cheese on top. "Hungry?"

"Yes." In so many ways.

"You're not supposed to say that until after I show you the ring."

I laughed as I watched him walk toward me. "Mm hmm. I see that happening. You've no doubt been won over by my collection of zombie shirts."

"You underestimate the appeal of women who like werewolves," Rafe said, setting the plates down and putting a hand on either side of my chair. The man loved pinning me down.

And I loved being pinned.

He nuzzled my neck and nipped at my ear.

Giving him a quick kiss on the nose, I disentangled, shooing him to the other chair so we could eat breakfast. The scramble was delicious, with a welcome layer of heat and flavor.

But there was one small problem: a gator was hiding under the potatoes. A gator with a blue and orange jersey, printed on the plate.

"Oh, Rafe..." I clicked my tongue. "I think I found out your deep, dark secret."

He froze for a second. Slowly lowering his fork he watched me with wide eyes. "What is it?"

"You went to University of Florida," I said in a conspiratorial whisper.

Rafe's eyes went wide and then he laughed. "Where'd you go?"

"University of Miami."

He gasped in mock horror. "Oh no! Our relationship is doomed! What religion will we raise the children?"

"They'll be Miami Hurricanes fans!" The rivalry between our schools was legendary.

"Oh no!" He laughed. "They'll be Gators. From little Gator onesies to college diplomas. They will be orange and blue all the way."

"Orange and *green*," I corrected.

Rafe's smile grew wider. "So we agreed on at least two kids and the color orange?" He winked. "My mother will be thrilled."

Oh, I'd walked right into that one. My cheeks burned. "Let's get through the first date before you start talking to your parents about me."

"Way too late," Rafe said. "Dinner at the food truck was our first date."

"That was just between friends!"

"Then we had a breakfast date," he teased.

"Random coincidence."

"Breakfast now..." He raised his fork. "That

means dinner tonight is our fourth date."

I took the last bite of my breakfast, which was as delicious as the man who'd cooked for me, and gave him my best stern expression. It was as intimidating as a hibiscus blossom.

Rafe laughed. "You sure you don't want to drive with me?"

"I'm sure." I took my plate to the sink, trying to dodge fragmented memories that ended in pain and abandonment. "Just... come home, okay? Cars always mean something bad is going to happen and it'd ruin my holidays if you got hurt."

"A drive over to switch cars with my brother isn't a big deal. I'll be home before you know it. You aren't cursed and neither are Decembers." Rafe set his plate in the sink beside mine and then wrapped his arms around me.

I relaxed into his embrace.

Did it scare me that he knew me so well? Maybe a little. But I was warm and safe in his arms, so I let it go. "I know... It's childish. Silly."

"So are clowns, and people are terrified of them." Rafe hugged me tighter. "It's okay to be afraid, Del. But I don't want you to be afraid alone. Even if you don't want me around as anything other than a friend and personal chef, keep me around for this. Please?"

"I will. Gator fan and all," I said, trying to laugh away my fear. Turning around, I put my hands on Rafe's chest and remembered he was shirtless and very, very fine as well.

His worried look turned into a boyish grin. "I love watching your face."

"Could you go find some clothes? You're very..." I ran my hands down his perfect chest. "Very distracting."

"And you don't need a little distraction right now?"

"I need to go get my laundry done so I have something to wear to dinner tonight."

Rafe stared past me for a moment, face suffused with pleasure. He licked his lips and looked down at me. "You know—"

"Let me guess. You know a place where I can eat dinner naked?"

He nodded eagerly.

"Uh huh," I tried to look serious. "Would dessert involve chocolate?"

"Would you like it to?"

I rested my head against his chest as I giggled. "You better go, or you might not make it out of the house."

Rafe's hand stroked my back. "Going to tie me up with those cute scarves you had?"

"Only if you want me to," I promised.

Oh, filters, where art thou?

It was a good thing Rafe was in a playful mood. If he'd pushed, I probably would have panicked, but he let me go with a loving smile and a featherlight kiss to the forehead.

"Hurry home so we can have our movie night?"

Rafe leaned in for a another gentle kiss. "I'll be home before you know it."

ANGRY GRAY CLOUDS STORMED UP FROM THE KEYS, rumbling and surging as they devoured the city. Heavy rain fell in curtains, pounding the street and drowning out every sound except the rhythmic whomp-whomp-whomp of the dryer futilely trying to beat the dampness off my bed sheets.

The owner of the laundromat sighed heavily as he flipped a magazine page with pictures of the Swiss Alps. He was the neighborhoods Pops, a tall black man with an easy smile and a Carolina accent that fell away when he started talking about his time living in central Europe. I knew for a fact he'd celebrated his eighty-fifth birthday every year since I'd met him. "Del?"

I looked up from my phone sheepishly. "Yes?"

"You going to be here all night?"

Rain lashed the window as lightning cracked the sky.

"I was thinking I might stay a bit."

My dryer dinged, signaling the end of the towel cycle and the end of my excuses.

Pops dipped his chin to look over his gold-rimmed glasses. "You want me to call you a ride?"

"It's fine. I can put the clothes in some trash bags." I hurried to match my actions to my words, scooping up my unfolded laundry and dumping it unceremoniously into the cloth carry bag. I could cover those with the plastic trash bags and it'd be almost as good as new.

"You eat today?" Pops asked.

"Yeah. Brunch with a friend," I said.

"Brunch?" He looked up at the clock.

The bright red numbers glared accusingly at me. It was after seven.

I smiled. "I... ah... It's fine. I have food at home," I lied. "And I had a snack before I came here." Telling him I'd gone home after a delicious breakfast with my new boyfriend and then taken a nap would only invite questions.

"You want a ride?" Pops asked. "I'm locking up anyway."

Stuffing the last load of laundry in, I smiled. "I got it."

"Suit yourself."

Thunder roared over Miami.

"You're going to get soaked."

"I have dry clothes at home," I said. It was true enough; by the time I got home, my dry clothes would be there and I could change.

It rained in Florida. A lot. It was part of life, like a hundred percent humidity in the summer, mosquitos, and tourists.

Schlepping my bags through the door, I caught a face full of cold rain. It was like stepping into an icy shower fully dressed. My flipflops slid under my feet.

I kicked them off, juggled the bags in one hand and reached to pick my shoes up.

My phone slipped from my purse, falling into a sunken puddle.

"Of course." I dropped the plastic bags and picked up my phone, shaking it off, for all that was worth. It buzzed in my hand and Rafe's number appeared.

Ducking under the awning of the closed pizzeria next door, I covered my left ear while I answered the phone. "Hello?"

"Hey, Del, it's Rafe."

"Yeah, I have your number saved. Are you home?" That would be the best news ever. Pops would let me sit in the laundromat for an extra ten minutes.

Rafe sucked in a breath and I knew I wasn't going to like his answer. "I'm actually still on 41. The car my brother sent back with me can't do the big highway. Or much of anything."

"How broken down are you?" He'd made it sound simple, a quick drive over to Naples, on the other side of the state along the Gulf coast, switch cars with his brother, and then home again. It was a four hour trip most days.

Unless the car hit a gator or broke down.

"I think it overheated, but—"

Lightning and thunder crashed overhead.

"Del?"

"Yes?"

"Where are you?" Rafe asked. "It sounds... loud."

"I'm just at the laundromat. It's a bit stormy out."

He cursed in fluent Miami creole, an amalgamation of English, French, Spanish, Arabic and Cantonese that was familiar to anyone living in our city. "The weather reports said the storm wouldn't be in town until tomorrow."

"The storm didn't read the report."

My phone crackled in the terrifying way that meant it was going to die.

"Rafe, I gotta go. My phone's dying. I'll see you tomorrow, I guess. Unless you get to town before midnight."

"I'm sorry, Del, I—"

My phone screamed, cutting Rafe off.

I turned it off and took the battery out, dropping it into one of my laundry bags for the trip home.

I was waterlogged by the time I hiked the two blocks to my apartment. Rain dripped off my hair, my nose, my toes... I was the swamp thing of Miami, glogging up the stairs like the living embodiment of monsoon season.

Hastily dumping my clothes into waiting laundry baskets, I sat on the floor and inspected my phone. Damp, but not broken. The protective case on my phone had cracked back in September. I'd meant to replace it, but never seemed to find the time. That's where the water had gotten in. Not much, but enough to seep under the plastic screen protector and into the ports.

Grabbing a mostly-dry pink towel, I did my best to shake the water out, clean the phone, and dry it off. Running the battery over the terrycloth one more time, I reassembled my phone and hit the on button.

It rang.

I blinked at the completely blank screen, listened to the ringtone of an unlisted number, and swiped where the answer button should have been, hoping to hear Rafe's voice. "Hello?"

"Del, my darling!"

"Mister Vietti?" I shook my phone as if that would somehow magically change the situation. "Hello?"

"Del, it's Vietti."

"Yes, I caught that. Sorry. I'm having phone troubles." I glanced at the clock on the microwave. "Mister Vietti, it's Saturday evening. The contracts office is closed. If there's an emergency, you need to call Mister Barros. I'm very busy at the moment. Happy holidays." I tried to end the call but the screen didn't light up or respond.

As I slid my thumb left across the screen again I heard, "It's about *us*." Vietti wasn't taking my very polite hints.

Sighing away from the phone, I smiled patiently and responded. "Mister Vietti, I've never heard of that piece. I'm on holiday and I'm having phone troubles. Please, call Mister Barros."

"Not a piece of work, Del! Us as in you and me," Vietti said.

"You and me what?" He didn't even sound drunk.

"Don't be coy, Del. I know our relationship hasn't been perfectly smooth or open, but that's why I want to get together tonight."

"No." Barros could take my end-of-year bonus and shred it. "There is no relationship here, Mister Vietti. I work at a company you sometimes employ to acquire and sell art. That is the sum total of our relationship." My hand shook as I squeezed my phone in rage. I was not for sale.

"That's not fair!" Vietti protested. "You flirt with me all the time. And I know you were flirting with Sionne last night. She sent me a picture of you wearing a dress you had to have bought with me in mind."

So, Vietti had slid into the use of hard drugs while no one was looking? Or was this just a bad trip from hallucinogenic edibles? "I was wearing an eighty-dollar dress I bought for traveling in," I said. "It's not special. It's not astonishingly impressive or expensive. I barely spoke to Sionne outside the sale of some mermaids."

When this was all over, I was going to have a good laugh about the ridiculousness of this situation. "Now, Mister Vietti, I am going to hang up and go fix my phone. You are welcome to call Mister Barros if you need anything else. Have a good weekend."

I took the phone from my ear, ran a thumbnail under the case and popped the battery out to end the call.

Right.

Now I needed rice.

And dinner.

And maybe something that would make me forget that that conversation had even happened.

What a crummy afternoon. I was all set to snuggle up to my new boyfriend and watch *Timberwolf Town*, arguably one of the best paranormal-horror series of the mid 20's, and instead I was alone dealing with calls from a rich idiot who thought being polite was the same thing as flirting.

I shuddered in disgust.

There was something wrong with the older generations of men. They were terrible at making friendships and always acted like any positive emotional interaction was a declaration of sexual interest.

Yuck.

I tossed my broken phone on my couch and looked around at the mess of my apartment. Did I really want to put on freshly dried clothes to run to the store? Not really. But I couldn't just stay home either.

Shimming out of my soaked shirtdress, I tossed it over the bar of my shower to drip dry, and considered my options. Delivery could work, but there'd be a holiday and weekend surcharge.

And it was just rain, after all. There weren't tropical storm-force winds or any safety hazards outside. It was just cold and wet.

Maybe running was the right option. I had some tight, black, dry-wick running shorts that wouldn't get too soggy even if I swam in them and a matching jogging bralet that doubled as a crop top. Well, maybe not in other parts of the world, but it was perfectly acceptable in Miami. Especially at Miami Beach.

With the running gear, I paired one of my favorite college fashion accessories: a broken iPod. With the earbuds in, I looked like I was in my own world, running to my music or podcast or audio book, but I was fully aware of my surroundings—and no decent person bothered anyone wearing earbuds. Florida had passed a law just after I graduated that made it a crime to bother someone who had earbuds in or headphones on, except in the case of an actual emergency or life-threatening situation.

The law did not say that the person with earbuds had to be listening to anything.

My key and bank card slipped into the pocket of my bralet. I pulled my hair back into a dripping ponytail and ventured outside again.

Gray evening had turned into the proverbial dark and stormy night. Cold rain cut across my skin. My running shoes slapped the puddles with a vengeance.

Thunder and lightning rolled around me like angry guard dogs, warning me away from their dark domain.

A nice zombie would have added an appropriately festive mood. Sadly, the local denizens of Miami were committed to their December activities.

As I pushed open the door to the bodega, fighting against a sudden gust of briny wind, a familiar voice sang out the familiar carol.

"Angel gettin' high. Shawty, she's my delight," I muttered along.

The old woman behind the counter looked up from her tabloid. A small tablet beside her was playing the highlights of some telenovela that had been new the year I was born. She frowned as she looked at the water rolling off me.

Smiling sheepishly, I hurried through the air conditioned chill as the angels continued to extol the virtues of the herbal life. Rice for the phone. A box of protein bars. A stack of microwavable meals that were shelf stable and good for another decade.

"Wild night?" the grandma asked as I put my purchases on the counter.

"My date canceled on me."

She rolled her eyes. "You want something more?" Her eyes darted under the counter to where she kept the 'naughty' magazines—the ones that made Maureen sigh and wonder aloud about the state of sexuality in America.[6]

I had to admit, skimpy bikinis and boys in Speedos didn't seem all that provocative when you worked with nude paintings all day. Plinths and cherubs were supposed to make it high art rather

---

[6] Maureen thought American tastes were still too conservative to be healthy. If you ever want a lecture on the difference between art, nudity, and seduction, Maureen has a three-hour lecture prepped and ready to go. There's a PowerPoint involved.

than porn, but there wasn't much difference at the end of the day. Naked is naked. And boring is boring.

"I'll pass." I held out my bank card and almost asked for a disposable phone. It wouldn't help. The only number I had memorized was 911 emergency services, and I'd have to lose my memories again before I dialed it.

"Happy holidays," the old woman said as she pushed my groceries into a pair of tiny canvas bags she charged me ten dollars for. They had Christmas trees and doves on them. "Bring your own bags next time."

"Yeah. I will."

It was impossible to jog easily while carrying grocery bags, so I didn't. I walked through the demonic night, letting the cold rain wash away my stress and anger until all that was left was the cold. The winds picked up as I turned down the final stretch of Ocean Drive. A big, black car zipped past, ignoring the speed limit and the puddles, sending a wave of street water over me. Maybe there was a bright side to the rain: as wet as I was getting, I wouldn't need a shower by the time I got home.

Lightning split the sky and, in the distance, a fountain of golden sparks heralded the ending of our power supply for the evening. The streetlights went dark and the neighborhood fell into a sudden, stormy silence.

Miami without the background noise of air conditioning, humming street lamps, and traffic is the soundtrack to a horror film. Trust me on this. There's nothing eerier than the sound of a city without the city noises. It's unnatural.

Shivering from cold and alone on the street, I started to whistle the first song that came to mind. Apologies to James Chadwick for liking the modern carol better. [7]

A car turned, coming toward me with the high beams on.

Cursing careless drivers, I turned away, waiting for it to drive by.

The car slowed to a crawl, blinding me with its unholy brightness. Someone tall stepped out.

"Del Farmer?"

I squinted against the light. "Who are you?"

"Craig. Mister Vietti is in the car. He wants to have a word with you."

A lot of appropriate responses ran through my mind, all of them variations on the intoxicated angel's favorite f-word. "I made it clear to Mister Vietti that I am not interested in speaking to him at this time, about business or anything else."

The bouncer-turned-hired-muscle made a grab for me.

I dodged. "Touching me is considered assault!" I said loudly, just in case there was anyone else out on

---

[7] For those without a wifi connection, James Chadwick wrote the carol 'Angels We Have Heard On High'. He probably wouldn't like the rap remix.

this god-forsaken night. "Forcing me into that car would constitute kidnapping and false imprisonment, and I have the right to sue for emotional distress and damages!"

Working with a legal team full of rotating interns gives a person a good understanding of the Florida legal system. And, at least in Miami, there were still people who were afraid of lawyers.

Craig walked over to the car, opened the passenger side door and spoke to someone inside. He turned to me. "Mister Vietti wants to talk."

"Tell him to dial a nine-hundred number." I walked past, circling wide of the car and stomping forward until Vietti's vehicle was obscured by the torrential rain.

My throat tightened with fear. Every instinct I had said I should run. But where? The beach would leave me isolated. The hotels would call the police on me before Vietti. Hell, half the Miami Good Ol' Boy club would say I was asking for whatever trouble I got into because I was wearing shorts and a running bra.

Behind me I heard Vietti's car start.

I walked faster, hurrying to the relative safety of my apartment. Just a quarter mile to go.

The car engine roared.

My back tightened, my shoulders coming to ears as I braced for whatever nastiness came next.

And the car drove off into the darkness.

Looking back, I surveyed the empty, rainy street with a grateful thought to whatever divine energy in the universe was looking out for me. Alone again, I shivered and suppressed a sniffle. Just the early signs of a winter cold, of course, not fear-induced tears. I wasn't shaking in terror because some random octogenarian had hired a brute to attack me. This wasn't the sixteen hundreds.

Habit made me reach for the pocket where my phone usually rested. But all I had was a broken iPod.

Zombie movies were better. At least zombies didn't have a choice when they attacked people. They weren't trying to eat anyone's brains because they were cruel or because zombies thought they deserved to eat brains. Vietti... I ran through all the things I'd ever said to him, trying to figure out where I'd gone wrong.

Then I shook my head, berating myself. I wasn't at fault. I had not attacked anyone. I hadn't paid anyone to fulfill some dark fantasy. This wasn't my fault.

Being pretty and walking home at night wasn't asking for anything.

Being polite to clients wasn't asking for anything.

Being a woman wasn't asking for anything.

I repeated the mantra I'd learned on the streets as I walked the rest of the way home. "Everyone is responsible for their own choices. A victim is never responsible for an attacker's choices. Everyone is responsible for their own choices..."

The rain fell in sheets of water like I was walking under a water sluice on a Hollywood backlot. Any moment, the music would crescendo into a lively tune full of optimism and the joy of... sitting in the dark?

"Dang it!" I kicked a chunk of concrete into the street as I realized the power outage combined with my dead phone would mean no binge watching anything tonight. There was no way my laptop was charged. I couldn't even heat up dinner unless I wanted to hold my microwave meals over a candle.

Looking both way down the street was useless, but I did it anyway. There was a glint of light a few blocks north or me, either a car or a cellphone, but too far away to matter.

My apartment was right across the street. I started across and too late heard the growl of a car speeding recklessly toward me. I froze, not comprehending— and was pushed to the side of the road.

I fell on the sidewalk, cutting my hands and knees, as the car thumped over something and moved on. The pain came first, a burning on my scraped hands and knees as the realization of what had just happened stole over me.

The car had almost... No. That didn't make sense.

Laughing weakly, I stood up, knees wobbly and hands clammy. It was an accident, nothing more. My defense mechanisms rolled into play.

I stretched out the shakes and forced myself to smile.

All this time I'd been wondering what movie I was in, and of course it would have to be the one where someone gets hit a few days before Christmas. "Santa?" I peered at the street. There was something dark on the road.

Abandoning my groceries, I braved the street again to see who had saved me.

The big black dog lay in the middle of the street, unmoving.

"No. No no nonono..." I dropped to my knees, defenses crumbling.

Running my hands through the rain-soaked fur, I tried to feel for a pulse, a breath, anything. He was warm under the mud and rain. "You can't die. I can't—No. You can't."

I ran my hands along him. Nothing felt broken.

Rain pounded the ground around us, isolating us, cutting us off from the rest of the world.

The dog breathed, chest heaving in and out.

He was alive!

"Okay. Um. Okay." I wiped anxious tears and rain from my face. "I can get you—"

Car headlights swept over me as the car turned.

"Inside. We're going inside." A protective, insulating layer of rage swept over me.

I picked the dog up, hoping I wouldn't damage his neck moving him, and sprinted for the safety of my apartment.

The dog lay limp and small in my arms. He'd seem so big earlier, full of energy and life. Now he seemed reduced. Shrunk.

Maybe he was just a very fluffy dog.

Propping his head on my shoulder, I dipped down to retrieve my grocery bags and hurried inside the gates.

Vietti's car drove past again, sweeping the night as he hunted me.

I watched from the shadows of the outside stairs as he drove past, then opened my apartment. It was pitch black inside, but I knew where everything was from memory.

Eight steps to the couch to drop the groceries. Twelve steps to the right of the couch was my bed. I tugged at the spare sheet I'd put down earlier, pulling it across my pile of pillows, and laid the dog there in the dark. Then back to the laundry bags for towels.

There was a battery-powered lantern in my nightstand and hurricane lamps in the kitchen, living room, and bathroom. I lit them, giving the small apartment a soft, golden glow.

I wished they'd give off some warmth.

The dog kept his eyes closed as I toweled him off, hot tears rolling down my face. He was breathing. There was mud and blood on him, but I couldn't find anything obviously broken.

Pushing my terror away, I tried to focus on what little first aid knowledge I had.

All I could think about was the poor bird who ran into our office window years ago. I'd been heartbroken, sobbing because I thought the little sparrow was going to die.

Maureen had scooped up the limp bird, put it in a box in the dark supply closet, and four hours later the bird had flown away as if nothing had happened.

Sometimes resting in a dark room was all that was needed for animals to heal. Maybe this was one of those times?

My hands were shaking. My whole body was shaking. I was... "Not good. Really not good. Come on, Del. Shower. Food. Water. Sleep. You know how to deal with this."

There were rules I'd made for myself. Wash off a bad day. Never go to bed hungry or dehydrated. Sleep it off before I worried.

My rules had kept me alive through the worst years of my life. Today didn't compare. In the morning, my phone would be dry, the power would be back on, and I could call Rafe. Or the police. Either way, by morning, this would be just another story to tell at a work conference when we compared the worst things rich clients did.

I showered by lamplight, scrubbing ferociously until all I could smell was the plumeria and plum of my body wash and the petrichor of the rain outside.

With the air conditioner off, the apartment was muggy and warm. Comfortably Miami.

There was a pajama set on the top of my laundry pile, a pair of little black shorts and a matching tank top bedazzled with the words 'Perfect Ghoulfriend'. Perfect. A protein bar and a glass of lukewarm tap water and I was set for bed.

Except my good blanket was still in the laundry bag. I set my dinner down on the side table and retrieved my pillowcases and blanket.

Making the bed with the dog sleeping there was impossible. I tugged at the sheet, trying to slide the puppy out of the way. He was breathing evenly and seemed bigger now, less wet and less likely to die.

Wrapping myself in my blanket, I eased myself into bed beside the dog, ate my dinner, and blew out the lamp.

The dog lay next to me, snoring softly.

I turned, trying to make out his shape in the darkness.

There was a canine sigh. The dog's eyes glowed with reflected light as he woke, lifted his muzzle, and licked my nose.

"Sweet dreams," I said. Resting my hand on his neck, I fell asleep.

I WOKE TO SUNLIGHT AND A STRANGE SENSE OF CALM.

It was weird. After last night, I expected my dreams to scare me into alertness multiple times during the night. It would have been normal for me to wake with my heart racing as adrenaline and fear flooded my system.

Instead I woke late, staring at the mid-morning sun flowing through the menagerie of glass fish hanging in front of my window. A rainbow of colors danced quietly across the stark white floor of my

apartment in time with the hush of the air conditioning.

There was a soft snoring behind me, a gentle
reminder that my puppy had survived the night.
Having a dog made all the difference. I'd slept so
well, even worried as I was about my furry rescuer.

Closing my eyes, I stretched out and reached to
run my hands through the dog's fur while I contem-
plated how I was going to explain all this to Rafe's
neighbor. "Hi, your dog ran off last night and got hit
by someone trying to run me over..." That wasn't
going to go over well. My hand landed on a warm,
smooth haunch.

No, that's not right.

I groped along the smooth skin, reaching for fur,
finding more skin.

There was a very human giggle beside me. "That
tickles."

Sitting up like a pop-up mummy in an old movie,
eyes wide open, I looked down at a very, very naked
Rafael Kane lying in bed beside me.

An ugly black bruise ran down his side, shoulder
to thigh, but it was still Rafe. Rolling. Stretching.
Frowning up at the mosquito netting and fairy lights
over my bed. His face creased in confusion.

"Um..." I shook my head. Rubbed my eyes.
Pinched myself. All the normal things one does when
one believes one is dreaming. Sure, I liked the idea
of werewolves. And the idea of Rafe in my bed wasn't
at all objectionable.

And I'd fallen asleep with a big, black dog in my bed. All those things added up to perfectly normal werewolf dreams.

Totally.

One hundred percent.

Completely normal.

A horn honked outside as I heard the crunch of the recycling truck scraping the side of the building.

Rafe rolled over, frowning. His gaze caught on my exposed torso and raked upward, a hungry fire burning in his eye.

"Um..." I swallowed hard. "Hi?"

So eloquent. Pure poetry. I was going to win awards for this conversation.

"Del?" Rafe sat up, eyes wide as he blushed and scrambled to pull the blanket over himself. Which left less blanket covering me.

Tiny shorts made sense when I was sleeping next to a stray dog. Next to a man, they seemed very... inadequate.

My heart beat faster. "Hi. Um... Oh. I said that. Okay." I ran my hands through my deranged beach-lady hair. "Is this a dream?"

Rafe a ran his tongue across his lips and narrowed his eyes. "Yes?"

I narrowed my eyes in response, joining in the suspicious stare-off.

"Can I get away with yes?" Rafe asked hopefully.

Once more, I ran through the sensory realities. Like a grounding sessions after a panic attack, I listed five things I could hear: neighbor's TV, the hum of the AC, the cars outside, seagulls, music from the bodega.

Five things I could smell: my plum blossom lotion, Rafe's expensive cologne, the earth-friendly cleaning spray in my kitchen, a lingering scent of chilis from the hall, the fresh laundry in the basket by my bed.

I could feel the soft bed under my fingertips, the cool air from the fan running across my skin, the heat from Rafe's body near mine...

"This doesn't feel like a dream." My dreams tended to have either full soundtracks or complete silence.

This sounded like reality.

But, I'd fallen asleep next to a dog.

Rafe looked away, projecting innocence while his checks flushed.

"I think, maybe, this would be a good time for an explanation," I said.

His head dropped, eyes averted in embarrassment. "This doesn't usually happen. I have very good control—"

"Ay!" I yipped in excitement and covered my mouth. "Werewolf! You're a werewolf?"

"Ahh, I mean..." Rafe lifted his head and frowned at me, looking confused and repentant. "I guess. Ish?"

"Hold on!" I jumped out of bed and rushed to my shelf.

Werewolf.

Werewolf.

Werewolf...

Where was my werewolf notebook? There. Dark blue with a silver halfmoon embossed on the cover over the outline of a howling wolf. Very practical. I grabbed my pen and ran back to the bed. "Okay. Talk."

Rafe looked down at my notebook. "What's this?"

"A list of practical questions to ask if I ever met a werewolf." I opened it to the first page where I'd listed questions in a sparkly, dark blue gel pen. "I don't want to be the stereotypical human who freaks out and faints when they see a werewolf. Or panics. So I made a list. I wanted to be prepared."

"To meet an imaginary monster that doesn't exist?" His worried look dissolved into a familiar smile.

I nodded. "Yeah. Except... you kinda do exist. Or this is a really weird and detailed dream." Yeah, no, not a dream. Rafe in my dreams was distant and disinterested. The Rafe in my bed was the man I'd talked about wedding rings with yesterday. The one with the warm smile and chocolate brown eyes. "So, let's start. Were you bitten or born this way?"

"Before we go on, can I use your restroom? Maybe eat something?" He sat up, looking at the kitchen. "Do you have food here?"

I looked guilty at my empty pantry. "Bananas and protein bars. And some microwave meals."

Rafe sighed in resignation. Obviously my food options didn't meet his culinary standards—which was no surprise, because they barely met mine. Wrapping the blanket around himself, Rafe climbed out of the bed and looked around with a frown. The oversized bed, the second-hand sofa, the stack of horror movies and the little bookshelf weren't at all interesting compared to his house.

No fancy art.

No comfortable couch.

Nothing remarkable.

Grim reality settled over me as he stomped off to the tiny bathroom.

The door slammed shut. The shower turned on.

I slumped back in bed. I knew I shouldn't have let him see the apartment.

Really, I couldn't blame Rafe for being disappointed. If I were a high-end art dealer, former model, and on several of Miami's Most Eligible Singles lists, I'd be disappointed waking up in this apartment too. I hugged my knees to my chest and tried to feel anything other than resigned.

This is what happened. People loved me until they saw the real me, the boring Del Farmer. I'd seen the real Rafe and he was still as handsome, smart, and captivating as the first time I'd seen him. He'd seen the real me, and was ready to run stark naked through the streets of Miami to get away.

Grumbling, I turned and flopped on the bed.

I'd just sleep.

That would solve my problems. I'd go back to bed and wake up tomorrow, hungry and empty, but sane. I could skip the whole post-relationship-depression.

The shower turned off. The bathroom door squeaked open, bringing a humid, soap-scented breeze.

The blanket shushed across the tiled floor as Rafe walked past my couch.

I waited for the front door to open and shut.

The bed bounced as Rafe flopped down beside me.

Turning my head to the side, I blinked at him. "You're still here?"

"Did you want me to go?" Big, chocolate brown eyes studied me.

"No." I shook my head.

He smiled. "Good. 'Cause I want to stay." He played with my hair, stroking it and tugging at it. "What are you thinking, Del?"

About how much I'd like him to touch me. About how much I didn't want this to be a dream or a passing phase. Because it felt like he really understood me, accepted me, and if he disappeared like everyone else in my life, it would destroy me.

"Del." His voice was deep, full of warnings and a hint of threat. "Why are you upset?"

I shook my head. "I'm not. I just... I'm processing. You're not going to run away, are you? Ghost me and pretend this never happened?"

"Running is not what I had in mind."

I planted my face in my pillow. "My house is terrible."

"Your house is you." He settled, the bed creaking under the extra weight. "It's very, very you. The neatly organized books and movies. The little pops of color. You always like art with lots of negative space. This suits you."

"That's not how I would have ever thought to describe myself." Or my apartment.

"It's cute. You have a notebook full of questions to ask a werewolf, should you meet one. I'm guessing the one with the bats on it is for vampires and the one with the kraken tentacles around the sailing ship is for any seas monsters that might visit Miami?" He laughed.

How had he...?

I pushed up on my forearms to look back at my bookcase. Okay, so the spines of the journals had the little pictures on them.

Rafe brushed a stray hair back from my face, drawing my attention back to him. "Are we okay?"

"I mean...." I lifted a shoulder and dropped it.

"Do you want me to answer your questions now?"

"Really?"

He nodded solemnly.

Sitting up and grabbing my notebook I flipped it open. "Okay, bitten or born this way?"

"Born this way. It's genetic." Rafe rested himself on an elbow so he could watch me write.

"If you bite someone, will they turn into a werewolf?"

Did I want to be a werewolf?

I hadn't thought about that. I flipped the page and scribbled the question down for later.

"No. No more than biting you would turn you into a Latina." He smiled and snapped his teeth at me playfully.

I frowned. "Is me knowing this going to get you in trouble? Is there some ancient and grumpy ol' wolf alpha who is going to rip out my throat if I tell someone? Are you going to get disowned for dating a human?" Worst case scenarios raced through my mind.

Rafe rolled onto his stomach laughing into the pillow. "Oh my—What?" He looked up at me. "What kind of horror novels are you reading about were-wolves?"

"The kind shelved in the paranormal romance section," I said without shame.

His expression changed from credulous to inquisitive. "Really?" His hand stroked along my thigh.

"I kinda have a thing for werewolves," I said, staring at his hand. He owned my heart. I'd fallen in love so fast, but I didn't know where we were going from here. "So, when you were talking about secrets…"

Rafe looked down at the bed, muscles tensing along his back.

"You kinda left this one out."

His jaw tightened and he looked away

"When were you going to tell me?" I didn't mean to sound needy, but I had to know. Had he kept it secret because he had to, or because he didn't trust me?

"Sometime between now and when I got you an engagement ring? I guess?" he said, still refusing to look at me. "I wasn't sure how to break that news. It's not something you can google."

"Yeah." My train of thought ran off, chasing the idea. "I can see why this isn't a first-date sort of topic. I mean, yeah, you need to bring up kids, and child support and drug convictions, but you really can't tell everyone you date you're a werewolf."

"It's not like the books. No one's telling me I can't tell my lovers. There's no alpha, or paramilitary pack, or mountain stronghold. But it's a hard topic to bring up in a casual conversation." He closed his eyes and laughed as if he was remembering something. "My sister wished there were packs. Teresa spent half of high school swearing she was never going to date a human boy. She was going to wait for a proper werewolf to sweep her off her feet."

"How'd that work out?" It was the first time he'd ever used his sibling's name and I was curious.

"She's thirty, single, and has threatened to literally kill me if I send her one more secret Valentine."

He rolled onto his side, face perilously close to my bare thigh. "Are you angry?"

"No." I shook my head. "I get it. We all have secrets." Even from ourselves. "How many of your exes actually know?"

"None of them." There was pain in his voice. "Miami's a very open society, but that's not something most people are prepared for." He frowned over at my notebook. "When you said you preferred werewolves I thought, I dunno, maybe? Maybe you knew? Maybe you'd known a werewolf before? Maybe you'd picked up my hints?"

"Hints?"

Rafe raised his eyebrows. "I told you my mother raised dogs when I was a kid, and that I got hairy sometimes."

I laughed. "That's not a hint that you're a werewolf!"

"I thought it was good enough." He kissed my knee.

"It's really not enough," I said. "We should get you some clothes and food. This is... It's magic, isn't it? Because you're not a huge dog. Big, yes, but not ginormous. Can you only shift at night? Is it moonlight? Can you actually control it?"

"Do you have a written questionnaire I can fill out?"

"That would be practical. Should I go get you a new notebook?" I turned, like I was going to get out of bed.

Rafe caught me, pinning my hip so I couldn't roll away. "I'm teasing, Del! I'm teasing. Uh, let's see... Yes, it's probably magic. No, none of us know the exact details. Yes, there are werewolves everywhere. It's like blonde hair or blue eyes, just one of those random genetic mutations, I guess? I can shift whenever but we get larger in the heat."

"And you live in Miami?" I asked dryly. "That seems practical."

"I grew up with the heat, so it doesn't bother me. I'm about the same size year round. But my cousins in Alaska?" His eyes went wide. "They shift down here and they look like some prehistoric monster that escaped a museum. They should be hunting mammoths. In Alaska, they're dog sized. And illegal in the Iditarod."

I raised my eyebrows. "I'm surprised that came up."

"Mm hmm, it counts as having an extra human helping with the race."

It was slowly dawning on me that he'd almost died last night. I'd almost lost him. I put my notebook down, more interested in Rafe than in answers. The bruise on his side was healing rapidly, but it was still noticeable. "How close were you to dying last night?"

Rafe laced his fingers with mine so I couldn't touch his side. "It's not as bad as it looks."

"It looks like you broke some ribs."

He lifted my hand to his lips for a kiss. "I'm alive, and I'm here, and I'm going to start chewing on the blanket if I don't get some food." He sat up. "Let's walk back to my place. I'll answer all your questions. Show you the family photo album. Break out the calendar."

"Calendar?"

He laughed and kissed me again. "Remember how I said I was a geeky teenager who related too well to werewolves on TV?"

"Yes…"

"The consistent thing there was that people freak out when they find out. Obviously, for some of us, relationships work out. But a lot of times when someone finds out they panic, and they run, and they wind up making excuses or doing drugs or all sorts of things to forget us. I've planned how to tell someone what I was for years.

"It was easier coming out as bi to my high school boyfriend. And I wanted to tell a couple of them. But there'd always be a point where I'd make a joke about werewolves or monsters and they all dismissed it. I remember watching the *Timberwolf* reunion special with my boyfriend and he said, 'Isn't that the most unrealistic thing ever? It's such a weird fetish.'"

I cringed.

Rafe's smile was tight. "We broke up a few weeks later. It wasn't the only thing wrong with the relationship, but it was a factor." He touched my cheek as he looked in my eyes. "Can you imagine what that's like? And what it's like to come from that to meet someone like you? You see a dog turn into your naked boyfriend and you have a notebook! You're not scared of me! So, you can see why I might want to lock this down."

"Plus, creepy old men try to kidnap me."

World's worst response to a marriage proposal. My brain seemed to have short circuited.

"There's that too." Rafe nodded. "We're calling Barros after breakfast. And then the police. Because if your creepy old stalker comes back, I will break more than his car."

I took a deep breath, recalibrating everything.

"Del? Don't worry about it. I'm not going anywhere. I'm staying with you."

That's all I wanted. Rafe beside me and a chance at happily ever after.

"Promise." He kissed my leg. Light as a breeze, gentle, teasing...

My mouth went dry.

Rafe lifted himself onto his forearms and shifted his weight so his arms were on either side of my hips and his body was between my legs.

He kissed the inside of my thigh and my heart thrummed.

He moved up my leg, dropping butterfly-light kisses as he climbed higher. Rafe looked up, a wickedly delicious smile on his face and his eyes dark. He moved upward, kissing my exposed stomach. Tickling me with his tongue. He reached my tank top and licked over the fabric.

My fists clenched the bedsheets as every muscle tightened in anticipation.

With a wink Rafe moved on, lips climbing my neck, kissing my jaw, nipping at my lips until I opened for him.

He tasted like my mint toothpaste. His tongue moved across mine and my back arched.

My blood fizzed. All I wanted was more.

"What do you think, Del?" I felt his smile on my lips. "Could I make you happy?"

"So, so happy," I assured him.

Rafe chuckled. "You're not worried about a werewolf nibbling on you?" He took a nip at my ear.

"Mmm, no. This werewolf can nibble on me all he wants." If he stopped now, I'd have to resort to begging. I'd forgotten how good it felt to be the center of someone's attention.

He fell back into the bed, pulling me on top of him with a smug smile. "Does this mean you'll grant my holiday wish, since I gave you what you wanted?"

I tilted my head in confusion. "I don't remember seeing your wish on the wall."

"It wasn't exactly work appropriate." Rafe's grin was delicious.

"Does it involve chocolate?" I guessed.

He nodded. "And New Year's Eve fireworks. And my shirt on the floor next to that wickedly divine little white dress." He ran his hands down my arms, tempting me closer. "And a midnight kiss…"

"How could I say no to that?" I ran my hands through his thick black hair. This is what I wanted, to have someone love me for who I was, zombies and all. I caught Rafe's lips between my teeth, tugging and licking, tasting him and drinking him in. I broke away with a smile. "Thank you."

"For which kiss?" Rafe teased, fingers tickling the back of my knee.

"For everything. For being you."

Loving brown eyes met mine. "Thank you for being you, and for loving me the way I am."

Miracle of holiday miracles, I smiled. "I do. I love you."

"I love you too."

ACKNOWLEDGMENTS

Books never come out of nowhere. They are a magical alchemy of hard work, wild ideas, and time generously donated by family and friends (who tend to get neglected while a book is being written).

I'd like to thank my support team for putting up with me while I worked on this. My husband, for being supportive. My kids for understanding that Mommy sometimes rambles about plot holes (and needs you to check her Spanish). My friends and crit partners for not rolling their eyes when I told them what I was writing. And my very patient editor, whose request for a holiday short story created a novella.

I love you all.

ABOUT THE AUTHOR

LIANA BROOKS loves spending her winter holidays surrounded by white sandy beaches, good books, and good company. She currently lives in South Carolina where the beaches are open all year, and fondly remembers her younger years when she went to Miami to read *The Odyssey* on South Beach. She loves beaches, but never really learned how to party.

When not surrounded by books, Liana spends her time hiking, playing near the river, and keeping up with her busy family.

Brooks is known for her space operas, including the *Fleet of Malik*, a series of connected sci-fi romances about re-building after a decades long war; and the enemies-to-lovers superhero series, *Heroes and Villains*.

You can find out more about Liana at her website, www.lianabrooks.com

She asked for a cosplayer. She got a supervillain who wanted to steal her heart.

Available from all major retailers.

THE POLAR TERROR

CHAPTER ONE

KADDY LEANED HER HEAD against the pale yellow wall of the hospital room, closed her eyes, and tried not to hear the constant whooshing and beeping of the machines.

The ticky-tick-tick of the heartrate monitor.

The two-minute beep as the IV dropped another controlled dose of pain medications that seemed to do no good.

The whock-whock-whock of the second hand on the clock.

There was no escape.

She couldn't even run outside to the snow and let that peace envelope her. Not while Everett was lying in bed, staring out the window at the flat roof of the parking garage, refusing to talk.

With a sigh, she tried to reach him. Again. "Do you want to watch some TV?"

Everett didn't move.

"We could play with your action figures." She pushed herself out of the uncomfortable chair and walked over to his bed.

Everett let her pull the plush Polar Terror doll out of his listless hand.

She bopped him on the nose with it. "The Polar Terror is coming! He'll walk right out of this storm and—"

Everett rolled to the side, crossing his tiny arms as best he could. His bottom lip quavered with anger and pain.

"I'm sorry." Kaddy put the doll back next to him. "We're going to find a way through this, Ev. I promise. And then we'll sew you the Polar Terror costume you wanted."

"There is no Polar Terror," Everett whispered, his first words all day. "Nobody comes to rescue you."

She rubbed his shoulder gently. "I know, bud. That's why you have me. You and me, we can handle anything."

"Not this," he whispered. "Not cancer."

Tears choked her. "We will," she whispered just as a softly. "We'll find a way to make it all right."

Everett squeezed his eyes shut.

Kaddy slumped back. Even if—and it was a really big if—the hospital pulled off a miracle and Everett got better, she wasn't going back to a job.

Her firm had been very patient, let her take a leave of absence, but her boss was retiring and the incoming boss hadn't liked her.

He'd questioned her education, her field time, her work ethic...

And while the guy couldn't come out and say it, his tone all but screamed SINGLE MOMS NEED NOT APPLY.

She shook her head. Being a single mom hadn't been her choice. She wasn't even dating when Everett was born.

But then there'd been a car accident a semester before graduation. Her sister and brother-in-law were killed on impact.

The idea of being a working, single parent was terrifying, but letting Everett bounce between foster families wasn't an option either.

Squeezing the guard rail of his hospital bed, she stood up. One way or another, she'd make a good life for him. That's what moms did.

There was a tentative knock at the door, like the person on the other side was hoping they wouldn't get an answer, but knew they would.

Rolling her eyes, Kaddy cracked it open for the inevitable nurse.

Andrea, the ever-perky Dream Coordinator for Merriton Pediatric Hospital, looked at her with the world's fakest smile, wide, frightened blue eyes, and damp blonde hair that looked like she'd gone outside without her usual hat.

"Yessssss?" Kaddy dragged the word out.

Andrea squeezed through the tiny crack in the doorway and slammed the door shut. "Okay. Hi, Kaddy! Everett! It is so good to see you two!" The words were rushed, panicked, and had the forced joviality of true terror.

But this was the Yukon in mid-winter, not some American city where a bomber was going to hold them hostage. "Is... is everything okay?" Kaddy asked.

The only thing that would scare Andrea was a really bad diagnosis. Kaddy's stomach flipped as tears welled. She couldn't handle that.

"Just dandy!" Andrea's voice squeaked. "Actually." She faked a laugh. "Funny story. Everett has a visitor. And, I know he's been so tuckered out, the poor thing, so I was thinking we should reschedule. Don't you? That's great!" she rushed on, not letting Kaddy answer. "I'll cancel. He can come back some other time."

Not bad news then.

Everett rolled over in his bed, forehead wrinkled in confusion.

"Who came?" Kaddy asked. The hospital attracted an eclectic group of visitors. Usually hockey stars, medical students, and politicians on goodwill tours. But Andrea welcomed them all with open arms. "It isn't the Maple Leafs again, is it?" No one this far north loved the Maple Leafs.

Andrea's head shook so hard Kaddy worried the woman was going to give herself a concussion.

"Okay..."

Kaddy glanced over at Everett who was showing

the first interest in anything since his chemo treatment two days earlier. "Is there a reason you don't want this person to see Everett?" She licked her lips and mouthed, *Is it child services?*

"Worse," Andrea whispered hoarsely. She leaned forward and murmured a name in Kaddy's ear.

Kaddy's eyebrows went up in surprise. "Like… for real? You—" She stopped herself just in time and leaned forward. "You found a cosplayer to play the Polar Terror?"

She couldn't keep the excitement out of her whisper. Everett was going to be over the moon.

"No." Andrea shook her head and glanced over her shoulder. The color drained from her face. "He's… he's not fake."

"Who isn't fake?" Everett demanded from the bed.

"Just say no." Andrea grabbed Kaddy's elbow. "Please?"

Kaddy shook the other woman off and looked at the door.

There was a thin layer of frost on the door. A suspiciously thin layer. Like someone was intentionally cooling the door for a grand entrance.

She narrowed her eyes. Would the Dream Coordinator come in here acting terrified just to sell the idea of a super villain at the hospital? Yes. Yes she would. It was *exactly* the sort of thing a perky, cheerful-before-coffee, former cheer-leader would do.

Kaddy crossed her arms and sighed dramatically. "I don't know, Andrea. Ev's had a really rough week. I don't think he should have visitors. Not even the Polar Terror."

The heartrate monitor screamed in excitement as Everett sat up like he was attached to a spring. "The Polar Terror?"

With a burst of cold air, the door fell inward. Ice crystals glittered as icicles formed on the ceiling.

That was some impressive special effects budget.

A man in the Polar Terror's costume stepped in, towering over even Kaddy, who hadn't been called short since she turned thirteen and shot up. The muskrat parka, a rabbit fur hat, a strip of seal skin, a fur pouch, beadwork on his boots... and of course the very modern black balaclava with the Under Armor logo.

The Polar Terror had come to Merriton.

Keep reading! Head to
[http://www.lianabrooks.com/ polar-terror/](http://www.lianabrooks.com/polar-terror/)
to buy your copy now!

BODIES IN MOTION
Fleet of Malik Book #1

A civil war tore them apart. Can a cold war bring them back together?

Available from all major retailers.
https://www.lianabrooks.com/fleet-of-malik/bodies-in-motion/

EVEN VILLAINS FALL IN LOVE
Heroes & Villains Book #1

Can a super villain at the top of his game drop everything to save the woman he loves?

Available from all major retailers.
http://www.lianabrooks.com/books/heroesand
villains/